Raves For
ROBE

MW00985416

"A surefire page-turner."
          —*Chicago Sun-Times*

"Dazzling."
          —*Michael Chabon*

"A master of his craft."
          —*Los Angeles Times*

"Perfect."
          —*New York Times*

"When Silverberg is at the top of his form, no one is better."
          —*George R.R. Martin*

"One of the great storytellers of the century."
          —*Roger Zelazny*

"Ferocious…brilliance comes burning through…
Silverberg's only hallmark is quality."
          —*Jonathan Lethem*

"Tight and thought-provoking."
          —*Locus*

"Robert Silverberg's versatile, skeptical intelligence controls
a lavish and splendid imagination."
          —*Ursula K. LeGuin*

"Grandly sweeping and imaginative…the sure hand of an
old master."
          —*Publishers Weekly*

He was a young man with good looks—but you had the impression that his looks were fading right before your eyes. The clothes that he was wearing were in the last stages of shabbiness, but they still bore signs that indicated they had been expensive at the outset.

Brady huddled over his drink and listened to the conversation of the young man and the girl, and felt lucky. They were talking about the very thing that had drawn him there that evening. In a way, that was natural enough, not really surprising. The affair was fresh in everyone's mind.

"I warned Doris," the drunk was saying, making dreamy circles in the water on the bar. "Not that it makes a damn bit of difference whether you live or die, not a single goddam bit of difference in this filthy kind of world we have to live in. They shovel you into the ground and that's the end of you, and it don't matter a damn who you were or what you did. But I warned her anyway. I warned her there'd be a rotten finish waiting for her." The drunk paused. "You know what? She's better off dead."

"What the hell do you know about it?" the girl asked.

The drunk scowled. "I know it's no good. Oh, it's all right when you've had everything else and hit the skids. Then you've got nothing to live for anyway."

"Like you, for instance," the girl jeered.

The drunk wasn't offended. "That's right," he agreed, his voice thick. "Like me. For me that would have been just fine. I'd have been a stand-in for her if the guy had asked me. All he had to do was come to me and say, I'm gonna kill somebody, bud, and you want it to be you or this girl here? And I'd have said kill me, I'm no use for anything, let the girl live. She's still got time to pull herself outa the mud..."

**SOME OTHER HARD CASE CRIME BOOKS
YOU WILL ENJOY:**

LATER *by Stephen King*
BLOOD ON THE MINK *by Robert Silverberg*
THE COCKTAIL WAITRESS *by James M. Cain*
THE TWENTY-YEAR DEATH *by Ariel S. Winter*
BRAINQUAKE *by Samuel Fuller*
EASY DEATH *by Daniel Boyd*
THIEVES FALL OUT *by Gore Vidal*
SO NUDE, SO DEAD *by Ed McBain*
THE GIRL WITH THE DEEP BLUE EYES
by Lawrence Block
QUARRY *by Max Allan Collins*
SOHO SINS *by Richard Vine*
THE KNIFE SLIPPED *by Erle Stanley Gardner*
SNATCH *by Gregory Mcdonald*
THE LAST STAND *by Mickey Spillane*
UNDERSTUDY FOR DEATH *by Charles Willeford*
CHARLESGATE CONFIDENTIAL *by Scott Von Doviak*
SO MANY DOORS *by Oakley Hall*
A BLOODY BUSINESS *by Dylan Struzan*
THE TRIUMPH OF THE SPIDER MONKEY
by Joyce Carol Oates
BLOOD SUGAR *by Daniel Kraus*
ARE SNAKES NECESSARY?
by Brian De Palma and Susan Lehman
KILLER, COME BACK TO ME *by Ray Bradbury*
FIVE DECEMBERS *by James Kestrel*
CALL ME A CAB *by Donald E. Westlake*
THE NEXT TIME I DIE *by Jason Starr*

The
HOT BEAT

by **Robert Silverberg**

A HARD CASE CRIME NOVEL

A HARD CASE CRIME BOOK
(HCC-155)
First Hard Case Crime edition: September 2022

Published by

Titan Books
A division of Titan Publishing Group Ltd
144 Southwark Street
London SE1 0UP

in collaboration with Winterfall LLC

Print edition ISBN 978-1-78909-992-8
E-book ISBN 978-1-78909-993-5

Design direction by Max Phillips
www.maxphillips.net

Typeset by Swordsmith Productions

Printed in the United States of America

Visit us on the web at www.HardCaseCrime.com

Introduction

I loved science fiction from the time I discovered *Planet Comics*, when I was seven years old, in the early months of World War II. I wanted to read all I could find about other worlds, voyages in time, strange alien beings. When I was a little older, and more interested in prose fiction than in comic books, I moved along to Jules Verne and H.G. Wells, and then to such science-fiction magazines as *Astounding Science Fiction* and *Amazing Stories*, which had gaudy, even embarrassing names, but provided me with an abundant supply of the fiction I most enjoyed. And, of course, since I had manifested a knack for words ever since I was a small boy, I wanted to write science fiction myself.

I wrote my first s-f story when I was thirteen or so—it was quite terrible—and went on writing them, and started to send them to the magazines I had been reading. I got them all back very swiftly, but once the editors figured out that they were dealing with a fairly talented boy rather than a demented adult, they sent me little notes of encouragement with each rejection, urging me to keep at it, study my craft, persevere in my ambition. Which I did, and when I was seventeen a magazine sent me a check instead of a rejection letter, and I was off and running as a science-fiction writer, just as I had dreamed of being since my earliest teens.

From 1955, when I was still in college, to 1959, I wrote one story after another, and sold them all, to *Astounding* and *Amazing*, to *Fantastic Universe*, to *If*, to *Infinity*, to all the science-fiction magazines of the day. It was a marvelous beginning to my career, and I never even thought of getting a real-world job when I graduated from college: I simply stayed home, wrote stories as fast as I could, filled whole magazines with my output. It was great while it lasted. But it didn't last.

There was a big upheaval in the business of magazine distribution in 1958, and many of the magazines I had been writing for suddenly went out of business. I hung on as a full-time science-fiction writer as long as I could, but after a time there weren't enough magazines left to support a prolific writer like me. I hunted around for new markets. One of my best s-f markets had been a magazine called *Super Science Fiction*, which began publication in 1956 under the editorship of an old-time magazine guy named W.W. Scott who cheerfully admitted that he knew nothing about science fiction, and, after I got to know him, asked me to help him out by doing a lot of stories for him. I was happy to oblige, and he bought every one, and gradually, as the s-f market started to vanish, I began writing for *Trapped* and *Guilty*, two magazines of crime fiction that he also edited. I had never been much of a reader of crime stories, unless you count the Sherlock Holmes stories, but I discovered that I had a knack for it and very quickly I was writing two and three stories an issue for *Trapped* and *Guilty*.

From there it was an easy jump to think about writing crime novels. During my time as a full-time science-fiction writer I had written half a dozen novels for Ace Books, edited by Donald A. Wollheim, and although Ace's s-f line was still going strong, I thought of branching out and doing crime novels for Wollheim's parallel line of mystery books. I proposed one for him, but he had plenty of good crime novelists in his stable and wanted me to stick to my established metier of science fiction.

During that time of professional uncertainty, though, I had begun writing for just about any market I could find, which included the booming men's-magazine market, publications with names like *Rogue* and *Venus* and *Mermaid*. One of them, *Exotic Adventures*, I wrote practically single-handed, four or five stories an issue, and when its publisher decided to branch out into paperback books, I was invited to write some for their newly launched Chariot Books and Magnet Books, at a fee of a thousand dollars a book, quite handsome for those days, when a dollar bought as much as ten or fifteen of our modern ones do. And so, in the spring of 1960, I wrote *The Hot Beat* for Magnet Books, a tale of urban low-life very far from my science-fiction roots but not all that different from the crime stories I had been doing for *Trapped* and *Guilty*.

As it happened, my career in noir fiction was a short one—I wrote two or three others, and then started writing non-fiction books on archaeological subjects that met with considerable success, and by 1965, as the science-fiction market returned to life, I wrote a couple of s-f stories at the invitation of a friend who was now editing one of the magazines, and wrote a couple more, and by and by found myself back to my first love, a full-time science-fiction writer again, which I remained until, having reached the age of three score and ten and then some, I chose to rest on my laurels and retire as a writer.

Much to my surprise, the old books, one by one, are finding a new existence in this new century. Nearly everything I wrote sixty-odd years ago has come back into print, even unto the stories for *Trapped* and *Guilty*, and even unto my long-forgotten Magnet book of 1960, *The Hot Beat*, now entering a new incarnation here in a time I once regarded as the far future.

Robert Silverberg
August, 2021

THE HOT BEAT

I

Just before midnight the thin December fog came slithering down from the hills to the city streets and spread a sickly haze over the ugliness of South Main Street. It left a film over the darkened store windows, and brought enough damp cold to make the tinny saloons which dotted the neighborhood look warm and cheerful.

The business curve of the fifteen-cent flophouses took a big upward swing. It figured. The stink and vermin of the cheap beds were lesser evils than the chill rawness of the Plaza benches.

The bums and floaters who had panhandled the price in the course of the day disappeared into the murky halls and up the creaking wooden stairs of a dozen of these rat traps. The others just continued on their way, wandering aimlessly.

Detective Sergeant Brady of the downtown station stopped to light a cigarette before he went into Carrol's Bar and Grill. With a cigarette dangling between his lips, he might possibly be able to affect a sort of casualness that could help to disguise somehow the cop which otherwise stood out glaringly all over him.

He cupped the cigarette in his hand, shielding the match against the cold wet wind. While he paused there, outside Carrol's, a middle-aged, stubbly faced tramp in a broad-brimmed Western hat came shambling up, already going into his spiel when he was five feet away.

"It's a lousy night, mister, and you look like you could spare it. Only a dime. Only a dime for one lousy cuppa coffee."

"On your way," Brady muttered. The panhandler seemed to

shrink back into the darkness. Brady pushed the blue enam-
eled door open and walked in.

The saloon was crowded.

Small parties of men and women sat in the booths near the
wall, talking and laughing noisily. A row of broken-down men
sat lined along the bar—drunks in varying stages of cheer and
despondency.

Five B-girls in cheap evening gowns sat on the high stools
scattered down the length of the bar. The deep necks of their
gowns revealed their breasts—some big, others scrawny. The
men clustered about the five allowing the bartender to refill
their glasses before their drinks were half finished. Down at
the end of the bar, one of the drunks was trying to put his hand
in one of the girls' dress-fronts. He got a good squeeze of a
breast that had seen better days before, giggling and squealing
shrilly, the girl pushed him away.

At the farthest end of the room, Sergeant Brady saw Carrol,
the proprietor, leaning against the big, shiny record player. The
juke was going full blast. Carrol glanced solemnly at Brady, his
face not displaying the faintest show of recognition. He covered his wide mouth with the hand that had been supporting
his chin, and watched as Brady squeezed in between two customers at the bar.

The man on Brady's right had one of the stools. He was fat
and sweaty-smelling, and he dawdled half asleep over his drink.
The man on Brady's left waved his hands about in vivid ges-
tures as he spoke. He was talking to the red-haired B-girl next
to him. The girl was the youngest of the five, and the open
front of her gown revealed firm, creamy young breasts that
hadn't yet acquired the B-girl sag.

He was a young man with good looks—but you had the
impression that his looks were fading right before your eyes. A

shock of straight blond hair fell across his forehead as he shook his besotted head. The clothes that he was wearing were in the last stages of shabbiness, but they still bore signs that indicated they had been expensive at the outset.

Brady huddled over his drink and listened to the conversation of the young man and the girl, and felt lucky. They were talking about the very thing that had drawn him there that evening. In a way, that was natural enough, not really surprising. The affair was fresh in everyone's mind, and Brady had counted on Carrol and the girls to steer the talk around it. Brady looked the man over from the corner of his eye.

"I warned Doris," the drunk was saying, making dreamy circles in the water on the bar. He shrugged sadly, his face taking on a bleary-eyed but philosophical expression. "Not that it makes a damn bit of difference whether you live or die, you know that? Not a single goddam bit of difference in this filthy kind of world we have to live in. They shovel you into the ground and that's the end of you, and it don't matter a damn who you were or what you did." He paused to belch. "No, it don't matter. But I warned her anyway. I warned her there'd be a rotten finish waiting for her if she didn't pack up and go home." He waved his hand again. "What kind of a life was that for a girl with her looks anyway? Selling her rear like a cheap floozie. Hell," he finished, "you know what? She's better off dead."

"What the hell do you know about it?" the girl asked in a surly voice.

The drunk scowled and tried to draw himself up straight. "I know it's no good. Not one goddam good thing about it. It doesn't lead any place. Oh, it's all right when you've had everything else and hit the skids. Then you've got nothing to live for anyway."

"Like you, for instance," the girl jeered.

The drunk wasn't offended. "That's right," he agreed, his voice thick. "Like me. For me that would have been just fine. I'd have been a stand-in for her if the guy had asked me. All he had to do was come to me and say, I'm gonna kill somebody, bud, and you want it to be you or this girl here? And I'd have said kill me, I'm no use for anything, let the girl live. She's still got time to pull herself outa the mud."

"You liked Doris, huh?"

He finished his drink before he answered. "Yeah, why not? Everybody liked Doris."

"For what she gave you?"

The drunk glared. "You got me wrong, sister. I wasn't interested in Doris for that. Oh, no. I was finished with all that, too—a long time ago. A…goddam…long…time…ago…"

His voice trailed off sadly and he looked out into nowhere, humming to himself.

2

Brady was aware that somebody was standing in back of him. He turned quickly, to face a round-faced, smiling man.

"Didn't know this was where you relaxed," the man said.

Brady forced a grin. "There's no sign up says only bums and columnists allowed."

The sleepy drunk on Brady's right turned his head to look at them. Apparently what he saw displeased him. He grimaced disgustedly, then rose and departed.

The round-faced man laughed. "People hate cops instinctively, I believe," he said. "It isn't natural not to, don't you think so?"

He sat down on the stool the fellow had vacated. He was a familiar figure in places such as Carrol's, third-rate hotel lobbies, cheap beaneries, Salvation Army posts, the police stations and the night courts. It was all part of a job which he held down on the *Gazette*, a job writing a unique column, sponsored by a liberal-minded editor who saw it as a counterbalance to the dry rot of prosperity and happiness which papers have to ballyhoo in order to hold their advertising. "The Seamy Side" was the title of the column and it did an excellent job of presenting just that but Lowry, its author, took nothing secondhand. To fill the column with what he wanted in it he had to keep moving around.

"I don't think about it," Brady said.

Lowry caught the glance Brady threw in the blond young man's direction.

"Still I'd give something to get my hands on the guy who murdered her," the young man was saying. "How could anybody have done such a thing? Strangled that lovely throat. My God, it was like a flower stem, so white, so graceful. It's horrible."

"Young love," Lowry muttered, hoping to draw Brady out.

"Or the ravings of the kind of guys they get down in the psychopathic ward," Brady said sourly. "You know, cry over a little white rabbit, then slit it open and cry some more."

Lowry raised his eyebrows. "Very scientific, Brady. Been reading Krafft–Ebing or something?"

"No, I'll leave the reading to you. I get to know a lot of the things you guys find in books and a lot more that you don't."

"Good for you. I was always strong for that first-hand experience stuff, myself."

"For cryin' out loud," the girl was saying. "I didn't know you were carrying the torch for her. She'd have laughed herself sick if she'd known it, I'll bet."

"Wrong again," the young man said. "Wrong on both counts. I only carried a torch once. I put it out in a barrel of corn. Since then beauty has been pure aesthetics with me."

"What's that mean?" the girl asked suspiciously.

Lowry couldn't suppress a laugh. The girl knew he was laughing at her. She leaned over to glare at him.

"You went to Harvard, I suppose, Mister," she snapped, "but I still don't like the way you're laughing."

Lowry's mirth grew uncontrollable. "As a matter of fact I did," he said. "And I'll try to laugh some other way."

The blond man wavered on his feet as he turned to face Lowry.

"Hello, McKay," Lowry said. "You're pure poetry and philosophy tonight. I couldn't help hearing you."

McKay grinned sheepishly. "Hiya Ned," he said. "Nice knowing you're around someplace. Old Faithful, the poor man's friend. Gives a fellow a sense of security. You been making fun of this little lady by any chance?"

Lowry laughed again. "Far be it from me," he said. "I've no quarrel with the uneducated. On the contrary, I think it's a blessing in disguise to be unable even to read. But laughing at her, good heavens, no."

"Then I've no faith in that sense of humor you're famous for," McKay said solemnly. "Because I tell you, Ned, this little lady, when you get to know her the way I do, is just about the funniest creature on God's green earth."

"Is that so?" the girl snarled belligerently. Her light blue eyes sparkled with anger. "And what do you think you're pullin', smart guy? I don't have to take anything like that from no stew bum like you."

With the back of her hand, she struck McKay on the cheek. He looked at her in bewilderment and then Carrol was at their side. He ignored Brady.

"Outside, you," he said to McKay.

A new aspect of the situation seemed to dawn in McKay's befogged eyes. From bewilderment he passed to a firm determination not to be the victim of an injustice.

"I'll stay right here," he said boldly.

"Like hell, you will," Carrol said. There was a burly man behind him now who seemed to be placidly awaiting developments.

Carrol put his hand out to grasp McKay's collar. McKay swung from the hip and landed a lucky punch on Carrol's jaw. Carrol went down. Somebody whooped with glee a little further down the bar. Carrol's husky assistant moved in to grip with McKay. The barfly who had shown such pleasure when Carrol was hit now flung the contents of a glass into the bouncer's eyes. Carrol's man wiped the liquid from his face with his palm, then shifted his attack to his new source of trouble, forgetting McKay, who grasped the advantage and let him, too, have one from the hip.

But Carrol was up now and rocked McKay with a blow that landed flush on his mouth, sending him to the floor. That should have ended it, serving as it did in place of the few more drinks that it would have taken to put McKay in the same position, but Carrol's lieutenant had made a serious mistake in now ignoring the man who had flung the drink at him. That playful lad picked up a half-empty bottle from the bar and greeted his adversary, at close quarters, with a sharp crack on the skull. Then somebody took it into his head to feel sorry for the bouncer and clouted the temporary victor. In another minute all but a few men, the girls and Brady and Lowry were in the thick of it. Lowry and Brady stood close to the bar and watched what they could see of the brawl. Somebody yelled "he cut me" which indicated a more or less successful stabbing. Brady eased himself over to the door and returned in a few minutes with two patrolmen in black leather windbreakers. The latter looked more like a couple of seedy building watchmen rather than cops on a big city force but they made up for the poor figures they cut with the zest with which they wielded their night sticks. A respect for the law, even if a little slow in coming, was restored and the two policemen took ten of the most troublesome in tow, just as the siren of the patrol wagon was heard outside.

3

Brady stooped down and yanked the unconscious McKay to his feet.

"Take this one too," he told the policemen.

They shook McKay into wakefulness and supported by one of the cops, he staggered along, rolling his head from side to side as if it were attached to his neck by hinges. The police who had come with the wagon met them at the door.

"That one was all right where he was," Lowry said pointedly.

"Which one?" Brady asked.

"McKay, the one you reminded them to take along."

"Friend of yours?"

"In a way. I knew him before he went to pot."

"Can't say much for your friends, Lowry."

They both started for the door.

"You didn't drop in just in the hope that you'd be in time for the brawl, did you Brady?" Lowry asked peculiarly.

"No, but I don't know why I'm telling you."

They walked down the street together.

"You didn't have to tell them to take that boy along," Lowry said.

Brady looked at him. "Say, what is this anyway? He belonged with the rest, didn't he, and besides what's it to you?"

"He's been having a tough time, for one thing."

"Cry about it in your column."

"For another, I have a feeling you wanted to take him in the first place, fight or no fight. Sometimes two men cross each other's paths and you know right off the bat that one of them is going to bend over backwards to make the other one miserable. There's no sense in it but it happens that way."

Brady's eyes narrowed slightly. His square, fleshy jaw jutted out a little further.

"Sometimes, maybe it's a good thing it's that way," he said. "Some guys need to be made miserable." He stopped abruptly and faced Lowry. "I got nothing against you, Lowry, but I've often asked why they let you run around loose all over head-quarters. You're not only too damn nosy, you're a pest."

"Thanks, Brady," Lowry said.

"Don't mention it."

Brady walked away quickly and turned the corner. Lowry strolled slowly in the direction of the *Gazette* Building.

In Dumas on Wilshire Boulevard, sleekly groomed men and women ate their midnight suppers, drank costly liquors and lis-tened to the orchestra's smooth rendition of a South American tango. Half a dozen couples danced in the semi-darkness, the women with frozen smiles on their faces, the men intent upon the steps they were taking. One of the dancers, a fortyish, bullet-headed man, pulled his partner toward him at the same time that he took a long backward stride. The awkwardness with which he executed the step made the girl laugh. He quickly relapsed into a series of more modest maneuvers which, if they made the dance look less like the tango, at least offered some degree of security from disaster.

"I was never much of a tango dancer," he said.

"You're doing very nicely," she said quickly, anxious to make him forget that she had laughed at his clumsiness.

He held her closer, pressing his fingers into her bare back. He looked into her eyes and smiled, displaying a mouthful of large teeth. She returned the smile, putting a softness into her calm brown eyes, then she lowered the long black lashes as if the intensity of his gaze were too much for her.

"You're lovely, Terry," he said.

"Thank you," she said. It was easy this time to restrain the impulse to laugh. The remark, she thought, was as badly timed as his dancing but a verbal clown is never as comical as one who actually tumbles about the arena. She hadn't trusted herself to think of a witty retort. The temptation to put a sting into it would have been too strong and besides a simple "thank you" smacked of the sincere modesty which she knew he looked for in her.

He led her about in a small circle, holding her more tightly than was necessary. She hoped the music would stop soon.

The orchestra let the number fade out on a series of soft measures. The man and the girl returned to their table. A waiter refilled their glasses and withdrew. They sat in silence. He opened his hand on the table and she put her own in it in a show of understanding. His eyes caressed her dark hair, the fine, even features, the soft bare shoulders.

"I feel as if something big is happening to me, Terry," he said. "I don't know how to describe it. I suppose it would sound silly. I'm supposed to be the man of action, you know, the extrovert. Ask anybody if he'd believe Jack Colin was ever anything else?" He paused, put into his face what was meant to be a wistful look. "Sometimes people with dreams in their hearts, people who could have been poets if they hadn't hidden their true natures from the eyes of the world, are forced into lives of action."

She forced herself to return the pressure of his hand.

"I've found something in you, Terry," he went on. "Something I've needed for a long time. It makes everything else look small by comparison."

Was it possible that anyone had ever swallowed a line like that, she wondered. Some must have. Those women who wouldn't notice the shrewd lines around his eyes, the bullish neck, the loose, flabby mouth. Perhaps they had even liked him without having an axe to grind.

"I'm glad," she said.

He rubbed her fingers with his own. Her hand was growing clammy from his perspiring palm. She saw him floundering for something with which to follow up.

A thin, sallow man approached the table. Colin looked up at him and frowned. The man barely looked at the girl.

"My God," he said to Colin. "It's a good thing there aren't twice as many joints in this town or I'd have had some more places to look. Where you been all day?"

"My partner, Mr. Rafael, Miss Stafford," Colin said. He looked sternly at Rafael. "Meet Miss Stafford, Sam."

Rafael nodded quickly in Terry's direction. Without waiting to be asked, he yanked a chair over from the next table and sat down.

"Look, Jack," he said. "You didn't say you'd be out all day. That's all right but at least you could have called up. I been in a spot and I didn't know what to do. Michaels—he's still waiting. He swears he's gonna tear up Shayne's contract and the hell with it if he doesn't sign right away. I knew you'd want to hold out but hell, fifteen hundred a week ain't beans and Shayne ain't as hot as he thinks he is anymore. I didn't know what to do."

Terry watched Colin's face grow hard. "I couldn't get back today. I don't want to talk business now, if you don't mind. I'll see you in the morning, Sam."

Rafael looked from Colin to the girl and back.

"Can that, will you Jack?" he pleaded. "The lady will excuse you." A wave of resentment made Terry flush as she caught the slur in 'the lady.' "I tell you Michaels means it. He won't wait till tomorrow."

Colin shook his head impatiently. "Please forgive this unwelcome interlude, Terry," he said pompously. "It's the price one must pay." He turned to Rafael. "All right, Sam. Go to Michaels. Tell him if he won't renew Shayne's contract at two thousand, he can go to hell. Tell him I said so and tell him that Apex'll be goddam glad to pay it. You must be an awful sap letting a guy like Michaels put it over on you. He knows damn well Shayne is worth two thousand to any studio in town."

Rafael looked dubious. "You really think it'll work, Jack? I'm not so sure."

"You're not sure! What do you know about it? Letting Michaels pull stuff like that! Who the hell's he think he's fooling around with?"

Rafael rose to go. "I hope you're right, Jack. I'll see you in the morning." A pasty grin spread over his face as he turned to Terry. "Good night Miss—or—"

"Stafford," Terry said shortly.

"Glad to have met you."

Terry saw him smirk at Colin as he turned to leave.

When Rafael was gone, Colin finished his drink. It restored him quickly to his former mood.

"It's as I was saying, Terry," he said. "Sometimes men have dreams in their hearts but the world won't let them bring those dreams to beautiful life. A man's soul doesn't really belong to him then."

Terry took a cigarette from the pack on the table. Colin held a match to it. With her other hand she held her glass. That left neither hand free for him to dampen with his moist paws.

"I understand, Jack," she said mechanically, feeling strangely stupid and uncertain that she could carry on with the game.

"I knew you would, my dear," Colin continued. "There's something fine about you that's different. You can see things like that where others can't."

4

She wished she could bring things to a head, ask for what she wanted and get it over with one way or another. But would it be wise to throw a wrench into the machinery now by dragging sordid materialism into the spirituality he was parading?

He looked vaguely about the half dark room and seemed to decide he could develop his mood no further in that atmosphere.

"Shall we go?" he asked suddenly.

She nodded her head in a way that told him his every wish was her command. They stepped out into the night. A sedan was waiting, a huge, black car half a block long. The chauffeur came scuttling out to open the door for her, and she slid lithely into the roomy back, nestling into a corner of the wide seat and staring straight forward at the black, sleek hair of the chauffeur.

Colin moved in close to her side. He slipped a hand possessively round her waist.

"You're so lovely, Terry," he murmured.

She forced herself not to blurt out, *Don't you know you said that a little while ago?* Instead she forced herself to smile, hoping he'd let it go at that.

He didn't. He moved closer to her, practically flattening her against the side of the car, and he pressed his rubbery lips on her mouth. At first her head moved back instinctively, then, fearing he would notice, she remained passively inert. She did not want to offend Colin.

His lips clung to hers. His hand roamed upward from her waist to her bare back, then began to wander past her left side until the groping fingers just barely touched the curve of her breast. She felt sharp inner disgust at the contact, but she did not remove the hand, nor did she give any hint of welcoming the caress.

After a moment that threatened to be prolonged forever, he removed his lips from hers, let the hand drop from her breast, and sighed deeply. She said nothing. He drew his features into the melancholy, faintly ridiculous expression which she knew was the precursor of more talk about his soul.

She looked out the window at the scattered lights along the boulevard. Colin leaned his head back against the soft, plushy upholstery and turned his eyes in the same direction. The car glided smoothly along, leaving Wilshire and beginning to climb into the low hills. The headlights played on a huge Chamber of Commerce sign at the side of the road:

FASTEST GROWING CITY IN THE WORLD.

FOUR AND A HALF MILLION PEOPLE NOW.

EIGHT MILLION BY NINETEEN SEVENTY.

Colin snorted contemptuously. "So what?" he asked rhetorically.

"I don't understand," Terry said, looking at him.

"That sign," he explained. "It gets me. Around here every damned thing gets interpreted in terms of figures. Eight million by nineteen seventy, the sign says. That's no promise, Terry. It's a downright threat. Another four million small lives grubbing for pennies. Everybody's values are all wrong in this city. In this entire country, for that matter. The beauty of existence is being crushed out by sheer numbers."

Terry tried to look interested. "You feel things too deeply," she said.

"I know," he said eagerly. "Don't you think I know? That's what makes it so tough."

She regretted instantly having displayed such warmth and understanding. He interpreted it as a signal for him to plant another kiss on her mouth.

Again the thick lips pressed hers. Again the groping hand went into action, only this time it snaked round her body until it could grasp her breast tightly. She was wearing a low-cut dress, and his sweaty fingertips pressed deeply, seeking the little stiff point of the nipple. At the same time his other hand rested briefly on her stockinged knee, then began to crawl upward, past the rim of the stocking, past the garter, to the soft satiny flesh of her thigh. Terry stood it as long as she could. Jack thought he was stimulating her by putting his hand between her legs, by groping for her breasts, but all she felt was sharp revulsion. She controlled her reaction, toning it down: all she did was slide her lips away from his and tactfully remove his hand from her bosom. The other hand wanted to remain in place; she slid it out from under her panties and pulled her dress back down over her knees.

Colin smiled faintly. She wondered if he thought she was simply going out of her way to make the chase more exciting, more of an erotic steeplechase. She looked out of the window again and noticed the direction in which they were going.

"Aren't you taking me home, Jack?" she asked evenly. It was hard to tell from her tone whether that was what she wanted.

He continued to smile. "Not right away, Terry," he said quietly. "Do you mind?"

"No," she said cautiously. "No, of course not. It's just that I'm—well, rather tired. I don't really think I'd be very good company."

He laughed lightly. "I can't imagine you being anything else, darling."

The car was pulling into the driveway that led to Colin's big, Norman-style house. Colin moved to kiss her again, as if to give her a tantalizing sample of the delights that were in store for her. This time, he twisted full around to face her, and both his hands went for her breasts, gripping them tight, cupping them in sweaty fingers, seeking to slip beneath the bra and touch the tender nipple.

She turned her head away and drew his eager hands from her bosom.

"Not now, Jack. Please," she murmured.

The car came to a halt in front of the house and the chauffeur hopped out to open the door for them. For a moment nobody moved. Her breasts still tingled painfully where he had grabbed her. After an instant Colin stepped out of the car and extended his hand politely, to help her out. She hesitated for a moment, afraid to spoil whatever chances she might already have built up for herself, yet unable to take the step that ought to clinch her position.

"I'd rather not come in with you now, Jack," she said. "I hope you don't mind."

He stiffened perceptibly, bit his lower lip. "Just as you wish, Terry," he said with dignity. He turned to the chauffeur who was standing by, "Aki, take Miss Stafford home."

He put his head inside the car, giving her a good look at the hurt expression on his face. "My man will see you safely home," he said.

"Thank you, Jack," she said. She wanted to say something else that would smooth over the abrupt denial in her decision but she couldn't think of anything.

"Good night, Terry," Colin said.

"Good night," she replied.

As the car swung down the drive again, she could see him slowly climbing the stairs, his head hung low. She knew he would play the part of the unhappy lover through as long as there was a chance that she was still looking.

She listened to the smooth hum of the wheels on the wet road. Had she bungled it, she asked herself. What else could she have done? It was one thing to make up one's mind that it was worth abandoning a few principles to gain an end but quite another to go through with it, especially with a man like Colin who not only left her cold but repelled her. Well, he might even look upon her behavior tonight as something that added zest to the affair. But if he did and called her again, then what? Could she get him to land her a screen test before she had definitely to show her hand? Thinking about it left her tired and sad. She closed her eyes and tried to put it out of her mind. When she looked out again, they were driving down darkened, almost deserted Hollywood Boulevard. A few late stragglers turned to look at the slinky limousine as it rolled by. Terry drew back in the corner, indifferent to the effect of the splendor in which she rode. The chauffeur pulled up in front of the apartment house in which she lived and opened the door for her.

"Good night, Miss," he said as she got out.

"Good night," she said mechanically.

5

She found her key and opened the hall door. Then she slowly climbed the flight of stairs and let herself into the one-room apartment. Her thoughts had depressed her until she seemed to feel a pain that was physical. She dropped her wrap on the divan that served as a couch and bed in one and walked over to a table on which stood a picture of a clean-cut, blond boy who seemed to look right back at her with a pair of gay, smiling eyes. She picked the picture up and looked long at it.

"If we could only have worked out our lives the way we should have," she said softly, "I could have done without all this gladly."

She took the picture with her and lay down on the divan. She held it up and continued to study the lively, smiling features. A sensation of deep pity for the boy in the picture, for herself, for the petty desire for fame as a substitute for the things she had really wanted, brought slow tears to her eyes. Holding the picture close to her, she closed her eyes, waiting for sleep to take her, and remembering....

How long ago had it been? Six months? A year? A year and a half? The time just seemed to blur, now that it was all over. But she could remember the beginning so clearly. She had gone out for dinner with—what was his name?—Mike somebody. Mike Jurgens, a bit player, a nobody who had appeared in three or four B-grade movies and who was giving her a big line about how much he could help her career.

They had eaten, and they had gone then to the Lafayette for dancing. A new band was there, a sensational outfit that was rising fast and getting plenty of praise—Bob McKay and his orchestra. A bunch of high-stepping youngsters who had risen right out of nowhere to conquer the big time in L.A.

Terry didn't know much about them, except that they were the current sensation. But before the evening was over, she knew a lot more.

They came in and took a table. The orchestra was hitting it up strong, practically at fever pitch in the frenzy of its excitement. At the head of the orchestra stood Bob McKay, young, blond, almost unlawfully handsome. His face was flushed and glossy with sweat, but his eyes were bright and gay and his fingers danced over the keys of the clarinet, weaving a wild, excited tune that climbed toward the stratosphere. Terry watched in amazement. She had never seen so much sheer dynamic energy locked up in one person before. Up there on the platform, Bob McKay seemed to be revealing his naked soul, flinging his inmost self out in torrid music.

She sat transfixed, not even noticing when her escort asked her what she wanted to drink. And then the number ended. It ended abruptly, as though cut short by a cleaver. Terry didn't know it yet, but that was a trademark of the Bob McKay group. The abrupt ending catapulted everyone into a silence of tremendous intensity—a silence to be broken in a few moments by the start of a new number.

She stared at the bandleader.

The bandleader stared back. His eyes swung round to meet hers as though drawn by magnetism, and for a long moment they gazed at each other. Terry began to tremble under the intense stare. But it broke, finally, as a waiter approached the bandstand with a tall drink for the leader. Gratefully, McKay took it from him, gulped it down eagerly, smiled at Terry, and turned around to swing into the next number.

And the next, and the next, and the next....

And then it was ten o'clock, and the band was taking its break. Terry sipped her drink thoughtfully. Beside her, Mike Jurgens was scowling angrily. She had hardly said a word to him since they walked in. She had had eyes only for the bandleader, Bob McKay.

Suddenly McKay appeared at their table. He was red-faced and he was clutching a drink.

"Hello," he said. "Mind if I join you nice people for a minute?"

"Not at all," Terry said eagerly, forestalling a grouchy protest from Jurgens.

McKay slipped into the empty seat. "Whew! I really need this drink," he muttered. "I bet I lose ten pounds a night up there."

"You really give everything you have, don't you?" Terry asked quietly.

McKay shrugged. "What other way is there?"

He finished his drink and signaled, and almost as though by magic a waiter glided up with another. McKay took it, laughing. "Little agreement I have with the management," he explained. "I take part of my pay in free booze every night. Keeps me going." He leaned forward, his face close to Terry's, while Jurgens glowered in displeasure. McKay said, "You're so lovely you must be in pictures. What have you been in?"

Terry grinned. "Nothing, yet," she admitted. "In fact, I'm still trying to get my first screen test."

"You're kidding!"

"Wish I was. But this town is full of starry-eyed hopefuls."

"I'll be damned," McKay mused. "Well, let me tell you right here and now—if you don't make the big time, and make it really *big*, I'm no judge of talent. You've got it, you know? You

just seem to radiate warmth and beauty and—and magnetism—"
He laughed. "I guess I've had a little too much to drink. You're
a complete stranger and I'm going on and on about you. I don't
even know your name, after all."

"It's Terry. Terry Stafford."

"I'm Bob McKay."

"Yes, of course, I know," she said.

"And I'm Mike Jurgens," Jurgens said coldly. "Just as long as
we're so chummy, I might as well introduce myself, too. I'm
Miss Stafford's escort for this evening."

"Hello," McKay said without interest.

"Mike's in the movies," Terry said. "He's been in *Dark Victory*,
and *Terror at Midnight*, and—oh, lots of films, I guess."

"Must have missed them," McKay said. He finished his
drink and scrambled to his feet. "Well, time to get back to the
old grind. Nice to meet you, Miss Stafford. Terry. And you,
Jurgens. Come hear us again some time."

McKay returned to the bandstand and within a few moments
was leading his orchestra in another round of frenzied melody.
Terry and Jurgens danced for a while, but Terry kept turning
around to watch the leader of the band, and after the third
dance Jurgens said abruptly, "Let's leave, Terry."

"Not yet."

"I want to. There's a jazz club on La Cienega I want to take
you to tonight."

"I like it fine here," she said crisply.

Jurgens glared at her. "I feel like I've got competition here."

"Maybe you do."

"Well, I don't like that arrangement. I want to leave."

"If you do, you'll leave without me," she snapped.

"That suits me just fine," he snapped back. He opened his
billfold and took out a five-dollar bill.

"Here," he told her. "Take a taxi home. Goodnight, Terry."

"Mike—"

But he had already stalked out. Terry looked after him in embarrassment and anger. Then, with sudden rage, she seized the five-dollar bill and tore it into tiny fragments. Then she found an empty table down front, near the band, and settled down to listen to Bob McKay.

Evidently he thought that Jurgens had gone to the rest room. But half an hour went by, an hour, seventy minutes, and still Terry sat alone. During a break in the music McKay leaned down from the bandstand and whispered, "What happened to Romeo?"

"He got fed up and left."

"What the heck for?"

"He gets jealous easy," Terry said.

"So he stranded you?"

"He gave me money to take a cab home."

"Damn nice of him," McKay said fiercely.

"But I tore the money up. Guess I walk home."

"Don't be silly. I'm through here in another hour, and I'll take you. Is that okay?"

"Don't inconvenience yourself for me, Mr. McKay."

"It's no trouble at all. Matter of fact, it's a sheer delight. And the name is Bob."

She waited, and the minutes crawled by, and then finally it was closing time, and the band was coming off the stand, and people were leaving. Terry sat alone in the darkened dance hall for a few minutes, and then McKay appeared, looking worn-out and drained of vitality. He was wobbling a little, and there was a drink in his hand. He finished it off and smiled at Terry.

"Let's go," he said. "The chariot awaits without, milady."

He had a foreign sports car, low and streamlined. As they got in, Terry said anxiously, "Do you think you're all right for driving, Bob? I mean—"

"You think I'm too looped to drive? Let me tell you, baby, it takes five times as much alcohol as I've had tonight to interfere with my coordination."

And he was right—he drove recklessly but with good control. On the way home, they talked. She told him of her so far unsuccessful attempt to crash the movies, and he spoke of his—highly successful—orchestral career. It had started in college, and he had just skyrocketed on to fame with mostly the same group. At twenty-eight, he was on top of the world, making a hundred thousand a year and worshipped by everyone.

And yet he was worried. The strain of such intense music-making was taking its toll on him. To keep going, he needed drinks. But they took their toll, too. He was tired practically all the time, now. His temper frayed easily. Sometimes he muffed notes from sheer fatigue. But, he told himself, he was going to fix things soon. He was going to take a month's vacation in Bermuda or some place tranquil like that, and when he came back he'd have all his old stamina once again.

They reached her house and he kissed her goodnight, chastely, and she went in. That night she was unable to sleep for sheer excitement.

It was love, she was sure.

How about him? Was he just amusing himself by driving her home, or was he as interested in her as she was in him?

It turned out that he was. Terry went back to the Lafayette the next night—alone—and McKay came down from the bandstand to take a couple of dances with her while his men got along without him. They went home again together that night. This time she invited him in, and they had a couple of drinks, and they kissed long and passionately, though they went no further.

And then the next night—

It was in the early hours of the morning. They had curled up comfortably on Terry's couch, listening to some old jazz records of hers, and suddenly McKay turned to her, his lips going to hers, his hand tenderly stealing up her body to caress the full swelling mounds of her breasts, and she felt something ripening within her body, something wanting to be taken, and she clung tightly to him. And he peeled away her clothing without a word, she making no attempt to stop him, because she knew that this was what she really wanted, this above all else in the universe.

And when she was naked, he knelt before her, gently kissing the pink tips of her breasts, and she felt the nipples growing stiff and hard, thrusting upward, and she felt a tension in her breasts that only the touch of his hand could relieve. He stroked her body as though she were a princess. And then he was picking her up, sliding one hand lovingly round her shoulders and the other underneath her, and he carried her into the bedroom.

She lay on the bed, watching him undress, eyeing his lean muscular body with pleasure, wondering what it would be like, to have him do away in a moment the virginity she had had so long. She hoped it would not hurt. He was naked, now, smiling, coming toward her, settling down on the bed, caressing her, and she felt his weight on her, but oddly she did not mind the burden.

She spoke only once:

"Be gentle with me, Bob. This is—my first time—my first time ever—"

He was gentle, and there was no pain as their bodies joined, only warmth and the overflowing sensation of fulfillment as he guided her through the motions, until she needed no more guidance, until the shattering wonderful climax. He spent the night with her. She did not feel shame for her action. This was love, she told herself.

The real thing.

All the next day her body tingled from the memory of his caress, and she could not wait until night. But finally night came, and they made love, and slept well into the day, and she cooked for him and then it was time for him to report to the Lafayette for warmups.

That was the way it went, as weeks stretched into months. Her body came to be almost an extension of his; when they came together in bed, it was almost always perfect. There was the understanding that they would marry, "one of these days" —no rush about it, so long as they loved each other.

But McKay's drinking became worse. He was expending more and more of himself, first on the bandstand, then in bed. He needed the drinks to steady him. But his temper was not steady. He quarreled with customers, quarreled with his band, quarreled with Terry. After a while the Lafayette replaced him. He got a booking at a less flossy place. But now he was on the skids. He no longer talked about marriage. Some nights he just never came home. When he did, he was drunk.

Terry dismally watched her love affair turning to ashes in front of her eyes. For months she had given everything to McKay, neglected the furthering of her own career, spent every moment with him—and now it was all coming to nothing. The way down was fast.

One night he came home completely drunk and wanted to make love. He groped clumsily for her, but he smelled so badly of gin and sweat that he repulsed her. She was wearing nothing but a housecoat, and he pulled her to him, his hand diving past the lapel to grip her breasts, and he said thickly, "C'mon, baby, let's make it. Get down on the bed and cooperate."

She pushed him away, but he came back again, seizing the housecoat and ripping it off her, and she huddled with her arms across her breasts, ashamed of her nakedness in front of him for the first time, because tonight he was a stranger to her. He forced her down on the bed and she locked her ankles together, determined not to give in to him, hating him. He seized her thighs, bruising the tender flesh, but she resisted him, and in his drunkenness he could not separate her legs. Then he began to twist her feet, and the pain was unbearable. She drew one foot back and kicked him in the chest, pushing him away. He sat down hard on the floor, looking surprised. Then he rose, coming menacingly toward her. He slapped her face and gripped her breasts tightly and when she rolled into a defensive ball he slapped her side, her neck, her back. Suddenly the liquor became too much for him and he slipped to the floor, weeping and mouthing obscenities and threatening to rape her when he recovered control of his body.

That night she broke up with him. She threw him out into the street, and he lay there sobbing till morning, and then he went away.

The golden hours were over. Terry had his photo and her memories, and nothing else.

Regretfully she tried to pick up the pieces of her life as it had been before the McKay episode. She had given him her virginity, and when she stared at herself in the mirror she wondered if she looked any different now, looser, coarser.

She heard that McKay had been pitched out by the members of his band, that all his money was gone, that he was living like a vagabond. She felt pity for him, and above all a feeling of sadness for what might have been. But she never made any attempt to get in touch with him. That would reopen old wounds, she thought.

But at night as she fell asleep, she thought of him, and remembered his gentle hands tenderly caressing her....

6

The blond, white-faced young man named Bob McKay lay sprawled out on the cell cot with his arms outstretched above his head and one foot dangling over the side so that his heel rested on the floor. His lips were parted, permitting the breath to come through his teeth with a low, hissing sound. His eyelids were not quite closed, and through the narrow slits the bloodshot corneas showed, giving him a ghastly, deathlike appearance.

At first he did not feel the Mexican's hand on his arm, but gradually the pressure of the man's grip and the force with which he shook him began to penetrate through his deadened consciousness.

"Huh? What?" McKay mumbled fuzzily.

The Mex said, "Hey, you don't want no coffee? Come on, hombre, you look like you goin' to die. *Por dios*, drink some coffee, yes?"

McKay looked up wearily from the cot at the brown face of the Mexican who stood over him with the tin cup in his hand. He turned his head slowly, surveying the cell and learning from slow impressions where he was. The other Mexican sitting on the cot near the opposite wall laughed loudly as he watched the growing bewilderment in McKay's eyes.

"Boy," he said happily. "You musta' had some load on, man."

"Yeah," said the Mexican holding the cup. "He had a load on, all right. I guess he don't feel so good now." The Mex grinned down at McKay. "Here. Ya better drink this coffee."

McKay raised himself on one elbow. His head throbbed wildly and shooting pains went through his chest. His nose and mouth felt numb.

"Here," the Mex said gently.

He put the cup in McKay's hand. The hand shook a little. McKay drank the hot, black liquid. It stung his mouth and throat, but it quickly made his numbed senses return to life.

"Thanks," he said gratefully after he had taken several swallows.

The Mexican shrugged. "*Por nada*. It's all right. Maybe you can do the same for me someday, huh?" He laughed loudly at his own feeble joke.

Drinking slowly but with growing appetite, McKay finished the rest of the coffee while the two Mexicans looked on in amusement. When he had finished, he turned and sat with both feet on the floor, cradling his aching head in his hands.

"You okay now?"

"Better," McKay said thickly. He looked up. "This the downtown can?"

"Yeah," the man who had given him the coffee said, grinning toothily. "It's the finest in the city. How you like her, huh?"

McKay smiled faintly and nodded his head in understanding. He heard a heavy footfall outside and looked up through the bars. A big, jowly man in a spotted, untidy blue uniform looked through at them.

"Let's go, you birds," he said in a flat, tired-sounding voice.

The Mexicans rose. McKay remained where he was for a moment, but one of the Mexicans nudged his arm and whispered, "You'd better get up when he says he wants you to get up. Otherwise you get hurt."

The cop put a key in the lock and opened the door, and McKay rose to his feet. The cop stood back to let the three prisoners pass in front of him.

McKay's knees felt weak and unsteady. He stiffened his muscles to keep them under control and followed the two Mexicans. They came into a room where a number of other men were waiting. McKay quickly lost interest in his surroundings and gave himself over to foggy memories and a brooding analysis of his predicament. He did not know how long he stood there and he was only dimly aware of the occasional movement and activity in the room. A few things came back to his mind in the semblance of reality. For the rest he continued in a vain probing of his stupefied consciousness. Then a hand was on his arm and he walked where he was led. There were others behind him as he went through a door and walked into a circle of brilliant light that blinded him and stabbed at his eyes as if he were looking straight into a summer midday sun. He could see nothing because of the frightening glare and he closed his eyes to shut out the pain. After a while, by narrowing his eyes to slits, he could make out the platform on which he and the others stood and a group of men who stood in the darkness below like dim shadows.

Among these men whom he could not see, stood Detective Sergeant Brady and Police Captain Hendricks and between them stood a little, middle-aged Filipino, quaking with fear. The small, brown man looked up at the men who were coming out on the platform to stand squinting in the glare of the lights, and it frightened him to know that he was expected to point out one of these men as a murderer. Captain Hendricks' words had a literal meaning for him and Captain Hendricks had said, "If you saw the guy, Ramirez, you ought to recognize him. If you don't, I know you're stalling because I'm not so sure you didn't kill the broad yourself. If you're stalling I'll make it hot for you. We're running every bum and rummy who comes in through the lineup. Sooner or later you're gonna see him. When you do, tell us, do you understand?"

Not that Ramirez had entirely understood the Captain, but when he had told his friend, Santillo, what Hendricks had said, Santillo had shaken his head gravely. Santillo had been to school and understood many things that he, Ramirez, did not know about. "That is bad, Jose," Santillo had said. "That is what I thought they would do all the time. It is a wonder to me that they did not take it for granted that you did it. After all the girl was murdered on the lot near your house and those police are always anxious to make trouble for us."

"But how can they?" Ramirez had cried in distress. "If I had done it would I have gone to them with the story? Has anybody ever known me to go around with white girls? I am not a young man. It would be unbelievable."

"That will not trouble them," Santillo had said. "They will say you came to them to turn suspicion from yourself. They will say anything if they feel they cannot find the guilty one and must pin it on you to save face. You must do as he told you, Jose. You did have a glimpse of the man who strangled the girl on the lot. Of course you did not have a good look at his face but you know that he was a white man. When you see him in that lineup there may be something in his movements, in the way he carries himself, that will tell you he is the one."

"But," Ramirez had remonstrated, "if I do that, I might point out an innocent man."

"You might," Santillo had said with a sad smile. "But if he is innocent, perhaps he will be able to prove it. Certainly he will stand a better chance than you if they decide that you are guilty."

Although Ramirez could not feel as cynical as his friend, he had feared for himself the more from the moment of that crystal clear presentation of his position. Now as he stood between Brady and the Captain, he was obsessed with a desire to remove forever any doubts of his innocence. Trembling, he scrutinized the faces of the men on the platform as they came on, stood still in the light and went out.

7

So far he had seen no one who even vaguely reminded him of the man whom he had seen from the window of his shack in the grayness before dawn, no one whose movement might be lithe and quick as were the movements of the man he had seen. He believed now with the Captain and Santillo that if he saw the man he would know him and in a quavering voice he answered the questions with which Hendricks reminded him from time to time of the task he had to perform.

"See him up there?" Hendricks would ask as a group of prisoners would come out and stand before them on the platform.

"No, no," Ramirez would answer, pitiably afraid that he was offending the Captain by taking so long to find the wanted man.

And now a new batch of men had come out. Two of them were Mexicans. Ramirez paid them scant attention, then looked at the third who was tall and lean and even lithe and this time it was Brady who bent toward him and muttered in his rasping voice, "Is that the guy, Ramirez?"

Then Ramirez' heart leaped as he transplanted the man at whom he was looking to the lot near his house and saw him drag the body of the girl from the front of the car and drop her on the ground. Ramirez began to feel dizzy as he saw the quick movement with which the man bent once over the body, then leaped back into the car to drive off. And then he was sure, for even the face, which until now he had been unable to remember, appeared before him and it was the face of the man on the platform. If those shoulders moved, if that back bent, Ramirez knew it would be with the sureness that he had seen in the early dawn of that terrifying morning.

"Is that him?" he heard Brady say again.

"Yes," Ramirez said. His voice sounded as if it were coming from somewhere else. It was higher pitched than usual and he could not control its shakiness. "Yes," he repeated, wondering whether he had been heard at all the first time and then to make it clear beyond doubt, he said, "Yes, that is the man."

He saw Brady look at the Captain and then he knew that the Captain's puffy eyes were studying him.

"O.K.," Brady said. "Come on along now, Ramirez."

Walking between Hendricks and Brady, Ramirez left the dark room behind him. They took him to another room, a small room with a hard, wooden bench and they told him to sit down and wait. He looked after them as they went out. When they were gone, doubts began to torture him. He could no longer remember what the man whom he had just pointed out as a murderer looked like. Why had he suddenly been so sure in that dark room?

Ramirez leaned forward on the bench, dropping his arms limply between his knees. His head began to ache violently. He propped his elbows on his knees and clutched his temples with his veined, calloused hands. What would they expect of him now, he wondered. With a tremendous effort he controlled himself sufficiently to look up at the door which the two policemen had closed behind them. Where had they gone? A picture of what they might be doing flashed through his mind, something Santillo had told him they did behind closed doors. Would they lead him, too, through that door? He stared at it, fascinated. Then he began to shiver as if he had a chill.

On the other side of the door which had become a symbol of horror to the Filipino, there was a short corridor. Then there was another door which led to a room, furnished with a wide wooden table and a number of unpainted chairs.

McKay sat in the center of this room and in a semi-circle before him stood Captain Hendricks, Brady, a plainclothesman named Harrison and a uniformed cop. McKay looked from one to the next trying hard from the expressions on their faces to learn what was about to happen to him and why. His head hurt from the previous night's drinking and aware though he was that something serious was happening, a lethargy possessed him which made it impossible for him to feel fear or any other emotion. As a result, insolence rather than the curiosity he felt was what the policeman saw in his face.

Hendricks drew down the corners of his mouth, furrowing his forehead into a somber frown. He leaned slightly forward and peered at the other man coldly.

"You're in a spot here, McKay," he said meaningfully. "I suppose you know that."

McKay shrugged. "It looks like a spot, all right," McKay said slowly.

Hendricks thought he detected a contemptuous sneer in the reply. His face darkened even further. His eyes were cold with hatred.

"That's right, McKay," he said. "And it's a damned tough one, too. The kind of spot that leads you into the gas chamber. Now suppose you tell us all about it, eh? That'll make it a lot easier for all of us. A lot easier for you too, McKay."

The insolent look in McKay's bloodshot eyes seemed to deepen as his gaze roved from Hendricks to Brady and slowly back to Hendricks. Arms folded, Brady watched him impassively.

"All about what?" McKay asked.

Hendricks grunted disdainfully. Cracking his knuckles with

elaborate precision, he said, "All right, McKay. You can stall if that's what you like. But just remember what I told you. You're only making it tougher on yourself. Did you know Doris Blair?" he asked, snapping the name out with sudden sharpness.

Understanding came to McKay with a shock. And then he was overwhelmed by a tremendous feeling that they could not possibly believe what they were leading up to. It was all some kind of joke, he thought. He laughed as if to share their good humor.

"Sure, I knew the poor kid," he said. "Why do you ask?"

"Just can the act, buster!" Hendricks barked angrily. "Poor kid, my left elbow! And you didn't only know her, you batted around with her a lot—didn't you, McKay? Answer me."

"That's a lie," McKay said with deliberation.

Hendricks' reaction was instantaneous. He slapped McKay's cheek with his broad palm. McKay's head snapped back sharply. His ears rang from the impact of the stinging blow.

Hendricks said levelly, "That's just to show you that I'm particular about who calls me a liar, McKay. I don't take crap from scum like you."

McKay's eyes filled with hatred.

"You're nuts if you think you can mix me up in this," he cried. "You're just looking for somebody you can work off your stinking sadism on, that's all. Whose idea was it to pick me up, anyway?"

Hendricks seemed about to slap him again. McKay tensed for the blow. Brady fidgeted as though slightly bored with the whole interrogation.

"It isn't an idea, McKay," Brady said tightly. "I was in Carrol's last night and I heard you shooting your fool mouth off in there. There are a couple of things you'd better be able to explain."

McKay moistened his lips nervously. Hendricks' bluster had

failed to frighten him, but there was something in the quiet, matter-of-fact manner in which Brady spoke that gave him a tight, knotty feeling in the pit of the stomach, something that told him he had cause for fear. Quiet menace was always more terrifying than noisy blustering. Memories of things he had heard, read, flashed through McKay's mind.

"Well?" Hendricks said. "You going to cooperate with us, McKay?"

"If you want me to explain anything," McKay said, "I'm going to want a lawyer, first."

Hendricks snorted. "There. And a minute ago he was playing dumb."

"You'll get your lawyer," Brady said. "And you're going to need one bad, damn bad. But first you answer a few questions."

"Why should I?"

"Don't make me have to answer that, McKay," Brady said. "Because if I have to explain reasons to you, I'm going to do it in a way you won't like. Now just get that goddam chip off your shoulder and give me some straight answers. You knew Doris, you and she were pretty pally, weren't you?"

"What of it?"

"Why'd you put her away? Were you just so tired of everything else that this was the only thing you could get a kick out of?"

"I tell you you're crazy, all of you," McKay yelled, his voice going shrill with anger and cracking at the top. "But listen, both of you. You can't bulldoze me with a lot of ridiculous suggestions. Maybe I don't have a fresh shave, but I'm not one of your wineheads that you can railroad right into the gas chamber without the guy even knowing what's happening to him. I know I didn't lay a finger on that girl. And you don't have a reason in the world for suspecting me."

"You talk like you won't need a lawyer. But you still don't talk good enough," Hendricks said grimly. "What's more, we got plenty of grounds."

"You're bluffing."

"Like hell we are. You were identified in the lineup."

"What?" McKay cried, startled.

Hendricks smiled. "Yeah, I thought that would make things shape up a little different for you."

"You're stringing me."

Hendricks shrugged. "You were identified by a witness on the scene, and that's God's own truth, McKay. That was no deserted shack on the lot like you thought when you killed the Blair girl. There was a guy in that shack saw you croak the girl, friend. And in a few minutes there'll be another witness here to tell us about you—the doctor whose car you stole to take Doris for that last joy ride." Hendricks' smile was triumphant. "Remember, McKay?"

Puzzled, McKay looked down at the floor. Hendricks put it down as a gesture of guilt and evasion.

"We got no time to waste with any wise guy stew bums, you get me, McKay?" he shouted. "Come clean quick, you understand?"

McKay shook his head slowly from side to side. Detective Harrison, standing just next to McKay, reached down and with a quick movement pulled the shirt front out of the top of the young man's trousers, exposing his abdomen.

"Now, tell it," Hendricks roared.

"I still say you're full of it," McKay muttered with an effort. He still could not believe that all this was happening to him, that he was in custody on suspicion of murder, that these grim, determined men were fully set on beating a confession out of him. It was like a dream, a fantasy that came out of a bottle. It was the kind of dream you had when you drank too much 50¢-a-gallon

wine. Only you woke up out of those dreams. The only awak-
ening out of this one would come in the gas chamber.

"You killed her," Hendricks said.

"Like hell I did."

"You're lying," Harrison said, as if to give himself some justi-
fication for what he was about to do. As McKay turned to face
this new accuser, something descended on his naked belly with
a dull thud. A horrible pain went through his viscera, his chest
felt as if it were cracking open, and his limbs from the groin
down stung as though they were being pricked with thousands
of needles.

Through gritted teeth he muttered, "No—I didn't—I didn't
touch her—"

Another blow descended. This one was three times as ago-
nizing as the first. McKay slumped down in the chair, his eyes
closed and his mouth open, giving himself over to the pain with
short, moaning gasps. A hand on his shoulder jerked him roughly
back into an upright position.

"That goes on, McKay," he heard Hendricks' voice saying as
though from a great distance. "That keeps on happening to you
until you learn not to lie to us. Now tell us why you did it."

"I didn't—"

"You aren't very smart, McKay. You're only asking for more
of the same. More and more and more. We'll break you down,
though. We've broken stronger men than you. You're just a
weakling. A punk who's been on the skids so long he doesn't
know which way is up anymore, and you think you're going to
hold out against us. Well, think again, McKay."

McKay said nothing, simply continued to gasp for breath.

Harrison waited for another signal. Brady looked on placidly.
Hendricks kicked McKay sharply on the shin. The fresh sting
of pain caused McKay's heart to contract so that he was sure he

was going to die, hoped for it as an escape from the ache of his entire body.

They hemmed him in, with their cold menacing faces. The bright light blazed down. "Talk, McKay."

"You can't hold out against us, McKay."

"We'll turn you into pulp, McKay."

"Talk, McKay."

"Talk."

"Talk."

"Talk."

The door opened and an officer put his head in through the doorway.

"That doctor's here," he said.

Hendricks nodded. Harrison tucked McKay's shirttails back into the top of his trousers, drew his jacket about him and buttoned it. Brady took a glass of water from the table and held it to McKay's lips. It merely splashed down over his shirtfront.

Hendricks went out. Harrison and the uniformed cop hoisted McKay none too gently out of the chair he was sitting in and walked him around the room. His knees buckled several times, and if they had let go of him he would have pitched forward on his face. But after a few moments he was able to stand upright again.

"All right," he murmured. "You can get your lousy hands off me now."

8

They released him, and he swayed for a moment, then got his balance. He looked dazedly at the men on either side of him, then the same insolent look as before came back into his eyes.

"I'd like to work on you someday," he said savagely to Harrison.

"I'll give you another lesson later," Harrison said. "So you'll know how."

They led him into Hendricks' office. A tall, dignified looking man was talking to the Captain as they came in. He turned and looked at McKay. He looked at him long and hard, then he nodded his head.

"Yes, that looks like him," he said. "Though of course it was dark and I was excited, so I shouldn't say definitely."

"I believe you can say definitely, Doctor," Hendricks said. "He's already been identified by another. You can't both be wrong." He turned to McKay. "This is Dr. Clayton, McKay," he said. "Remember? Your memory's so damn weak. You know what you did? You lay down in the back of Dr. Clayton's car and waited for him to come out of a patient's house and then you stuck him up and took the car away from him because you needed a nice car to take your pretty girlfriend for a ride in. Remember that, McKay?"

Dr. Clayton stepped closer to McKay. "Possibly if I could hear his voice," he said to Hendricks. "I could tell. I'd hate to pick the wrong man, you know."

"Speak up, McKay," Hendricks said. "Dr. Clayton wants to hear what a rat sounds like."

"Wasn't it you who held me up from the back of my car?" Dr. Clayton asked lamely.

McKay shook his head slowly. "I don't know what you're talking about," he said. His voice was only a little higher than a whisper.

"Is the fellow hurt?" Clayton asked Harrison. "He hardly seems able to speak."

"Drunk," Harrison said. "He was picked up with enough liquor in him to have killed a horse."

Clayton returned to the Captain's desk. "Well, of course it's hard to say. If I could hear his voice normally, I believe I could tell."

"Well," Hendricks said impatiently. "He looks like the man who took the car from you, doesn't he?"

"Yes, but as I said, it was dark and I was excited. I really hate to say for certain. Can't you identify him from fingerprints on the car or something like that?"

Hendricks smiled benevolently. "Only a sap would have left prints on that car. He used it to drive the girl out to the lot where he murdered her, you know. He was smart enough to wipe the steering wheel and the doors clean of prints. Now, look, Dr. Clayton, you saw him, didn't you? He must have been right close to you if you gave him your money. Why should you have any doubt about it?"

"I don't know," Clayton replied irritably. "It's just that it was dark. People often get false impressions in the dark, especially when they're excited. This is serious. I don't want to involve a man who might be innocent."

"But you will say that he looks like the man who held you up."

"Yes, he does."

"O.K. Dr. Clayton, that's fine."

"Look here, Captain," Clayton said sharply. "This isn't the

beginning of a lot of calls to come down here, is it? I haven't much time, you know, and really I'd rather forget about the whole business."

"Don't worry about that," Hendricks said reassuringly. "We won't bother you any more than is necessary."

"I wish you wouldn't," Clayton said.

He started for the door, then with his hand on the knob he turned and looked at McKay. Somebody pushed the door open from the outside and Clayton stepped aside and went out past the man who came in. It was Ned Lowry. He smiled genially, then saw McKay and pulled himself up short. McKay grinned feebly at him.

"Hello, Ned," he said.

Lowry nodded curtly, quickly grasping the inadvisability of establishing friendliness.

"Nothing for you, Lowry," Hendricks said. "Mosey around somewhere else. We're busy now."

"Just as you say, Captain," Lowry said but he sat down on a chair near the wall. Hendricks gave him a dark glance, then motioned to the detectives to take McKay out. When McKay looked at him again, Lowry raised his eyebrows questioningly. McKay understood and shook his head. The simple message got across. "I don't know any more about it than you do," it said to Lowry. Lowry saw Brady watching him and forced a smile. In Brady's eyes he read a challenge. McKay was led out.

Hendricks made it clear that he intended to ignore Lowry. He bent over a sheet of paper on his desk and proceeded to look busy. The hint was wasted on Lowry.

"Rather special attention you're giving the drunks these days, Captain," he said, "or is it just that you're always nice to celebrities."

"Who's a celebrity?" Hendricks growled.

"McKay. Perhaps I should have said was."

"What kind of celebrity—or is the fact that you know him enough to make him one?"

"It's been known to happen. No, McKay had a big-name orchestra. *Dance the hours away with Bob McKay*, remember? Don't tell me you stay home nights, Captain."

"Not if I can get out, but I don't dance when I go out. I like short cuts. Why haul a dame all around the floor first?" Hendricks grinned maliciously.

"The subtle approach, eh Captain?" Lowry asked amiably. "Swell story for me in McKay. How the mighty have fallen and all that, you know. Could I see him?"

"The hell you could."

"Thanks. That's what I thought. What have you got on him?"

"Murder," Hendricks snapped. "Now go haunt a house or something, will you?"

"Murder," Lowry said. "I understand that's serious."

"It used to be. There's nothing to it anymore. They just put you to sleep now, you know. Like an operation. Don't even feel it."

"Very pleasant."

"Too damn pleasant. Hanging, now, or the chair—there's something else again."

"Something you can get your teeth into, eh? Substantial capital punishment."

Hendricks grinned. "Yeah, but the lethal chamber—like ether before they take your tonsils out."

"Sissy stuff."

"Right."

Hendricks bent over the sheet on the desk again.

"I couldn't see McKay, could I?" Lowry asked.

"I said no," Hendricks said without looking up.

"Murder, you said. Do you mean somebody was killed in the brawl at Carrol's last night?"

"You were there, huh?"

"Made a special point of it."

"No, a real fancy job. Doris Blair."

It was no surprise to Lowry. He had simply wanted to make certain.

"Did he confess?"

"Police business, Lowry. Now beat it, will you?"

"I was just going." He started for the door, then turned and looked solemnly at the Captain. "Have you been getting much exercise lately, Captain?"

"No," Hendricks replied without thinking. "What for?"

"I was just thinking," Lowry said slowly. "If you decide you need any, don't take it on McKay. I've heard tell of such things."

Hendricks shot a withering glance at Lowry but the bland eyes that met his held a quiet threat in them that made the Captain uncomfortable.

"So long, Captain," Lowry said pleasantly. Hendricks grunted.

9

Another day rolled by for McKay, marked only by the rhythmical questionings and beatings. He lay on the cot in a cell which was his alone now, his body a mass of bruised and tortured nerves, his brain afire with confusion and resentment.

The next day they had him in District Attorney Ford's office and here the tactics were subtler, wider in range. Most questions met with obstinate resistance and eventually Ford wearied to the extent where he sprawled in his chair behind the desk and lit a cigarette.

"You can't bluff us, McKay," he said. "We've got everything but your motive and we'll get that too, mark my words. I'll line it up for you and you can see that you can't bluff us. You were intimate with the girl. Your landlady, Mrs. Duncan, saw you leave the house at four in the morning." Ford stopped abruptly, hoping a surprise question would work. "Where were you going at four in the morning?"

"Where I told you," McKay answered quietly. "To El Centro to look for a job."

"Pitching alfalfa?"

"Yes."

"You expect anybody to believe that?"

"Yes."

"You, a musician who never did anything harder than blow on a clarinet, were going to break your back pitching alfalfa?"

"Yes."

Ford sighed wearily. "You're a liar. I'll tell you where you went at four in the morning. You looked around for a good, reliable car, one that you could count on taking you where you wanted to go and getting you away in a hurry. You found Doctor Clayton's car but the key wasn't in the switch—so you got a better idea and waited in the back of it. When Clayton came out, you pointed a gun at him, made him hand over the keys and took his wallet because even though that wasn't your real objective you figured you might as well grab the cash. Where did you put the gun?"

"I didn't have a gun."

Ford leaped out of his chair. "Then you admit that you hid in the car and held Clayton up."

"I didn't say that."

Ford sat down again. "You forced Clayton out of the car and then you drove it off and waited for Doris Blair to come out of Carrol's. You picked her up and drove off to the lot. You strangled her and pulled her body out of the car and left it in the weeds. The Filipino who lives in the shack on the lot saw you do it. And he saw you get back in the car and drive off. Then you left the car on a street three blocks away and disappeared for a couple of days. Where did you go?"

"None of those things happened," McKay said. "I was in El Centro those few days."

Ford banged his fist on the desk. "You're a liar, McKay," he shouted. "You were identified by Dr. Clayton and by the Filipino." He rose to his feet once more and pointed an accusing forefinger at McKay. "And I'll tell you why you murdered Doris Blair, too. It was because you were jealous of her. You thought she was tearing around with other men. You know you were and you let that vicious temper of yours get the best of you—that same vicious temper that made you hit the bottom —that same vicious temper that made you lose job after job until nobody would have you. You murdered Doris Blair when that temper got the best of you, just as you once broke a man's jaw when you worked at the Lafayette, just as you once smashed a violin over the head of one of your musicians, just as you've always resorted to violence when anyone has crossed you." Ford paused dramatically, looking for the effect of his oratory.

McKay straightened up in his chair. He surveyed Ford contemptuously. "I thought you said I waited for Doris," he said. "That I had planned her murder. How would temper enter into a situation like that?"

"Very clever, McKay," Ford said ominously, then he banged his fist on the desk again. "But I'll tell you why. Because you had only to look at her to be reminded of your jealousy and to feel the rage that comes so easily to you."

McKay smiled faintly, accentuating the look of scorn on his face. Ford shifted from one foot to the other uncomfortably. Then he motioned to the guard who had brought McKay there to take him out.

Back in his cell, McKay lay on the cot again, worn with the unending hurt of his battered body and the unutterable weariness of his ragged nerves.

And wherever he felt the sudden twinge of a pain, he immediately began to see and feel again the blow that caused it, to experience from beginning to end the shatteringly humiliating punishment.

Hatred for the men who had beaten him seethed inside him, and suddenly something seemed to explode where the turmoil had been and he screamed like a madman, a long high frenzied wail.

A guard opened the door of his cell to quiet him. McKay, maddened, sprang forward.

"Filthy bastard," he gritted. "Teach you to beat a man up—"

And, falling on the astonished guard, McKay struck the man

a fierce blow behind the ear. But the guard spun away, recovering himself, and with a quick slap sent McKay sprawling down to the hard floor. The next moment the cell was full of other guards. McKay dimly heard them talking.

"Tough guy—tried to break out."

"We better fix him so he don't get no more fancy ideas along that line."

They hauled him to his feet. McKay stared frightenedly into cold, ugly eyes.

The clubbing which followed left him mercifully unconscious for hours. When the doctor finally pulled him out of it, McKay would not talk. He would not move from his cot. He would not touch the unmentionable soggy food that was brought him in rusty metal trays.

He lay in a sullen stupor, closing his eyes, losing himself in a dream world where a lovely girl with clear brown eyes and firm, warm breasts soothed the tired ache of his body and held his head tenderly cradled in the sweet-smelling cleft of her bosom, against those ripe, delightful swells of rounded flesh, and then she opened her blouse to him and he buried his bruised face between her breasts, and their silky warmth took away all the pain, all the humiliation and agony, and there was only peace and calmness and love….

He stirred uneasily. A guard doing his rounds heard him muttering thickly, "Why, Terry? Why…?"

10

In the meantime, Ned Lowry tried repeatedly to get into the cell to have a talk with McKay. But Hendricks, shrewdly suspecting that there was plenty more to Lowry's interest in the case than the mere desire to pick up a good story for his column, made a special point of seeing to it that what could easily have been arranged was made impossible. But the papers had the side of the story which the police and the District Attorney's office had given them, and Lowry, sitting in his office scowling behind his typewriter, felt a pang as he remembered McKay's worn, handsome face and knew that the certainty of conviction of which the papers spoke so confidently was, indeed, a certainty.

It was a foregone conclusion. Lowry was able to visualize the public defender going through the mere motions of a defense that was no defense, just a hollow mockery of the due process of law. He could see it over and done with, whisked through the courtroom in jig time, quickly but not without pain.

Lowry lifted his big, well-knit frame out of the chair, snatched his hat from the rack, and went out, alerting his secretary to keep the office under control until he got back. Lowry walked four blocks to a tall office building and went up in the gleaming elevator to the tenth floor.

There he stopped in front of a frosted office door which said, in commanding gilt letters, PETER J. REYNOLDS, ATTORNEY AT LAW.

Lowry went in.

A decorative young receptionist in a tight yellow jersey smiled at him and said, "Yes, please?"

"I'd like to see Mr. Reynolds."

"Do you have an appointment with him, sir?"

"I'm afraid I don't. But I think he'll see me, if he isn't too busy. The name is Lowry, Ned Lowry. Yes, the one from the newspaper."

The girl looked momentarily impressed. Rising, she puffed out her chest in what was probably an attempt to give the famous columnist a good look at her cleavage, and said, "I'll see if he's free, Mr. Lowry."

"There's a good girl."

She disappeared into an inner office. But she returned in a moment.

"Mr. Reynolds will be glad to see you, sir."

"That's swell."

She ushered him into Reynolds' private office.

Reynolds looked fat—though not disfiguringly so—smooth, and competent. He put on a pair of pince-nez glasses when he saw Lowry and smiled.

"I'm glad to meet you, Mr. Lowry," he said in a full, resonantly commanding voice that was probably marvelous in the courtroom. "I've been reading your column for a long time, you know. It's an impressive job, I've always thought. Very impressive."

"Thanks," Lowry said without warmth. "It's always good to know that your work is appreciated by someone of some caliber. But I don't particularly enjoy writing it at the moment, however. It seems pretty useless."

"Sorry to hear that. Though I don't really understand what you mean by your column being useless."

"I mean that I try to help the people I write about. And just now I see an opportunity to help someone, but I can't do a damned thing. That's why I came to you, Mr. Reynolds. Perhaps you can help me."

"Would you explain?"

Lowry moved forward in his chair and stared levelly at the lawyer. "I came here, Mr. Reynolds," he said simply, "because you're supposed to be the best lawyer in town. Are you?"

Reynolds laughed at the blunt question. "Do you want me to be modest or honest?"

"Honest."

"Honestly, then, I am."

"Nothing less will do for what I want," Lowry said. "Now, to be blunt again—would you pitch in with me to help a poor sucker who is being railroaded into the gas chamber for a crime he didn't commit? I mean, would you insist on your usual fee?"

"It depends," Reynolds said good-humoredly.

"On what?"

"Well—if I like the case and if there's money, I take it—the case and the money— preferably as much of the latter as I can conveniently get. On the other hand, if I like the case a lot and there's no money, I may still take the case as a test of my professional abilities. But if I don't like the case at all, it's no go for me either way."

Lowry nodded, "Clear enough and well put."

"I assume there's no money involved here?"

"You assume right. There's no money except what I'll put up for expenses. But you'll like the case, because it's a tough one. A real challenge."

"I always enjoy a challenge, Mr. Lowry. Give me the details of the case."

"It's Bob McKay. You know about it?"

"Only what I've read in the papers."

"Looks bad, doesn't it?"

"Pretty bad."

"He's innocent," Lowry said with firm conviction. "Completely innocent."

Reynolds shrugged. "That's not unlikely. It's been known to happen."

"I don't want it to happen this time. I like that boy. He doesn't deserve to end up in the gas chamber on a railroad job."

Reynolds leaned back, thrusting his thumbs into his waistband and looking interested. "Well," he said, "I know the prosecution's angles. What are yours? Then we'll see. I don't want to take on a lost cause."

"McKay's young, about twenty-eight or maybe twenty-nine. He's a musician, a hell of a good one. He plays the saxophone and clarinet like nobody's business."

"I'm familiar with that."

"He started a band of college kids a few years back and raised them right into the big time, right up to the top of the heap. They were good. Too good, as a matter of fact. McKay worked like the devil. Inside of absolutely no time at all, his orchestra was generally rated among the best swing bands in the country. McKay was averaging two thousand and better a week for himself. But it must have been a strain."

"I imagine it was."

"In that kind of work, you know, the drinks are right at hand with which to relieve the strain. It's no trick to reach out and take a highball off a tray, when they're on the house. So McKay drank. Too much. And he began to get into trouble."

"What kind?"

"The night club kind," Lowry said, shrugging. "You know. Fights with customers, fights with bosses. He hauled off and broke a customer's nose one night because the guy was drunk and making insulting remarks about the band. Then a couple nights later he took a poke at the owner of the club. That finished him there, and the same thing happened at the next place. He started to lose jobs and the orchestra began to go down with him until one of his boys decided that the best thing for the good of everybody concerned was just to pitch him out on his butt before he wrecked the reputation of the entire group."

"And so they pitched him out?"

"Exactly. That and the drinking did a lot of damage in a short time. It's the old, old story. You've probably seen a hundred clients go to hell the same way. His money was gone inside of six months—naturally he never saved anything, never invested it, put it all into fancy cars and high living—and pretty soon he was down there grubbing on South Main Street with the rest of them. Probably all he needed to be saved from the slopheap was a little break from somebody, but you know the way that works. There's nothing that the boys and girls love better in the world than to kick a has-been in the teeth."

"Agreed."

"So he moved into a cheap furnished room someplace, and spent whatever money he had cached on booze in the dives. And, of course, that's how he got snarled up in this whole stupid murder mess. He knew that girl, sure. But so did I. A lot of people knew her. He was just the easiest one to get at. You couple that with the ridiculous coincidence of the identification by the two witnesses and there he is—walking down the last mile without anybody giving a damn that he's innocent."

"It's hard to argue against the circumstantial evidence," Reynolds said thoughtfully. "You're absolutely convinced that the man is clear?"

"Positive."

"How do you figure it?"

"Simple. He *couldn't* have done it. I know the boy, and it doesn't figure with his character. For one thing, I'm morally certain that his relationships with Main Street women never went a step beyond a conversation over a drink. He wasn't the type to get into bed with floozies no matter how low down he sank."

"A lot of men have high, moral feelings until they land in the gutter," Reynolds said. "It's easy to stay away from cheap dames when you've got lots of dough in your pocket. But when you're down and out, and the girl says she'll go with you for two or three bucks, it's hard to resist, wouldn't you say?"

"Not for this lad. He was shot through with idealism once, and no matter how much else of his past life went to hell I'm sure that part stuck. There was a girl he simply worshipped, once. A real beauty. Starlet, you know, but not your typical would-be Marilyn who'll put out for anybody important. She was badly gone on him too, but she let him skid once he started to." Lowry scowled. "Maybe she tried to help him and it didn't work. I don't know. Anyway, she packed in, and I know that hurt him as deep as you can hurt a man. But he didn't throw that overboard. I know that."

"You're a good judge of character, Mr. Lowry. I'm willing to believe that everything you feel about this McKay fellow is valid. But it's another thing entirely to make subjective character analysis stand up in court and convince a jury."

"I know, but I'm going to try," Lowry said. "Will you take the case?"

"I think so," Reynolds said. "Yes. Yes, I'm with you, Lowry. Goddamn, but I haven't had as stiff a challenge as this in years. I'll take it just on your say-so that the boy is innocent."

"I knew you would," Lowry said, extending his hand across the desk. Reynolds took it. There was a power in the fat man's grip that belied the flabbiness of his big body.

"Thanks," Lowry said. "We'll see him, then, and I think the

next thing will be to stall until I can dig up whatever I can." He moistened his lips anxiously. "If I can't dig up anything substantial, what would the defense be like?"

Reynolds shrugged. "We'll see that after we've talked to McKay. I can't plan in the dark. What are you figuring to look for?"

"Just hoping I can uncover some snags in what they've pinned on him. They're banking on pretty coincidental evidence, and I ought to be able to poke some holes in it if I work at it."

"Let's hope so, Mr. Lowry."

In the shadow of Reynolds' prestige, Lowry, too, was finally able to get to McKay. The imprisoned man was a chilling sight, with his bruised, swollen face and his dully staring, embittered eyes.

McKay sat on the cot with his back propped against the cold wall. He was haggard and pale, the bruises standing out in livid contrast on his face. He hadn't shaved or bathed in a long while. It was hard to see in him even the ghost of the once impeccable band leader that had existed.

At first he was somewhat indifferent to Lowry's visit. But it soon penetrated his fogbound mind that the two men were friends, and he began to thaw out.

Reynolds said, "Starting from the beginning, Bob. When you left your place that morning, where did you go?"

"I had heard that the trucks left early," McKay replied in a weary, defeated-sounding voice. "I went down to the produce district and stood on the road to wait for a lift."

"And you got one?"

"Eventually."

"Who with?"

"I got picked up by a truck that was going down to El Centro,"

McKay said. "Oh, yeah. There was another fellow got the lift with me."

"Splendid. It's vital to prove you were where you say you were. Do you know his name?"

"Wilson. Mack Wilson."

"Did he say where he lived?"

"Not the exact address. But he did say he wanted to move out of the neighborhood he was in because of his kid." McKay was silent a moment, trying to force his alcohol-soaked mind to disgorge the memories of that morning which seemed so many hundreds of centuries ago. "Yeah. I remember. I remember him saying it was a block of crummy wooden shacks on the other side of the river."

"Good. Now, when you got to El Centro, you didn't get a job, I suppose?"

"No."

"Did you stand in line at the ranch offices for any length of time?"

"Sure."

"And did you happen to talk with any of the men who were hiring?" Reynolds asked. "Did you leave your name on a waiting list, or anything like that we could use as proof?"

"No; I never even got to one of them. There was no hiring. And no waiting list to sign. We were just told to stand around and wait in case it turned out that they needed more men than they already had."

"But they didn't?"

"No."

"Did you talk to any of the other hands who were trying to get work that morning?"

McKay nodded. "Yes."

"Were there any you think we might stand a chance of locating?"

"No. We simply talked about work, about how bad times were when a guy had to apply for a chinchy job like this and just stand around and wait. I don't know where any of them lived."

"I suppose not," Reynolds said sadly, mentally crossing off that line of approach. Changing the subject, he said, "Bob, did Doris Blair ever tell you anything about herself?"

"Only that she hated the way she was living, wanted to get out of it."

"And that's all?"

McKay smiled feebly. "You got to remember that I was very rarely in a condition to remember everything she told me, of course. But I really don't think she told me more than that. How she hated the way she was living. She knew she should be doing better with herself."

"Who were her friends?"

"I don't know."

"Were they the other girls who worked there?" Reynolds wanted to find out.

"No. I'm quite sure they weren't. They didn't like her very much."

"That's the truth," Lowry put in. "She was rather superior to the rest of the lot and she made them feel their inferiority."

"Offensively?" Reynolds asked.

"No, it was unconscious on her part. She was just a girl with class. She showed them up for the cheap dyed-haired floozies that they were, just the way a Federal bill is going to show up a bunch of lithographed counterfeits if you put them side by side."

Reynolds' lips narrowed.

McKay said darkly, "They're gonna put me in the gas chamber, aren't they?"

"Not if we can help it," Lowry said.

By the time Reynolds and Lowry were ready to leave, McKay

was a little buoyed up, although obviously his experiences with the law had left him deeply pessimistic about his chances of ever escaping from their sticky clutches.

Outside, Reynolds shook his head gravely. "I don't like it much, Lowry."

"You don't think he's got a chance?"

"I didn't say that. As long as he's on this side of the gas chamber, he's still got a chance. But it'll be hard, Lowry. Damn hard with those two witnesses for the prosecution and the little McKay has to tell. You get an average jury of nincompoops who just want to tell their grandchildren that they sat on a murder trial, and they'll send him to his death without even biting their nails. Hell, he's practically convicted in the newspapers as it is. The jurors are going to walk into that courtroom already convinced that they're only going through the motions of a trial. That's what I'll have to fight against, Lowry. And I can't do it without some solid evidence to back up his story."

Lowry shook his head. "El Centro is out," he said. "That would be a sort of needle in a haystack search, especially the way the men keep moving in and out down there. But I guess this Mack Wilson fellow he mentioned is first on my list, at any rate. A block of crummy wooden shacks on the other side of the river. There are plenty of those but the post office might help."

Reynolds nodded. "If you could track down Wilson somehow, that would help. We may have something in that case."

"May?"

"Yes. Because of course he also has to be a reliable witness. You can't put a safecracker on the witness stand and expect to impress a jury."

"I'll see."

Lowry's next stop was at the post office. After bringing into play some high-pressure tactics that he had perfected in his everyday job as a reporter and columnist, he succeeded in getting the address of the man called Mack Wilson.

He drove quickly to a part of town which, though it is really nothing but a slum area, manages by virtue of the small ramshackle houses and the sorry-looking trees which grow here and there at the edges of the cracked sidewalks to look like a rundown suburb.

The address Lowry had gotten proved to be a vacant house. His heart sank. He could practically visualize the Fates, three old crones weaving the fabric of a man's destiny and refusing to be thwarted once they had mapped it out, laughing mockingly at him from whatever far-off place they inhabited. Their devilish plans to doom an innocent man had been made so carefully that not the slightest scrap in his favor could materialize. Lowry wondered whether his efforts would be of any use. Maybe it was just futile to go to all this time and trouble to save a man who was so obviously marked for the refuse heap of humanity. Even if he saved McKay through some miracle, what guarantee was there that the young man would not immediately go back to his old haunts and rapidly wind up either once again in jail or in some downtown alcoholic ward?

Then he felt low for having weakened so easily. McKay was a human being, he thought, and his life was at stake. He had no right to judge the way McKay chose to spend his life. But if it was in his power to save that life, he could not abandon the attempt until all hope was definitely lost.

With a determined step, he went to the door of the next house and knocked briskly.

A slatternly woman of about forty opened the door halfway. She eyed Lowry with cold suspicion, as though he might be a bill collector or a city marshall.

"Yes?"

"I was wondering," Lowry said, "if you could tell me where the Wilsons moved."

The woman shrugged. "How would I know?" she whined. "They didn't move anyplace much in particular, if you ask me. Mrs. Wilson told me they were going off to Orange County someplace to look for work. Picking peas, I think she said. They might be most anyplace by this time. Folks move around a lot."

Lowry did not dare follow up with any further philosophical conclusions about the craftily laid plans of the three wrinkled sisters. The combination of events and circumstances conspiring against McKay was so overwhelming that he did not dare think about it at all. He knew by now that whatever other information he might be able to secure would only serve to make everything look a good deal blacker than it did already, if that were possible.

"Tell me," he said, as she began to show signs of impatience with him. "Do you know whether they're likely to be coming back here?"

She gestured with her shoulders. "No, I don't, mister. But I kind of doubt that they will, you know. He had a pretty tough time around here, that fellow Wilson did. I mean, being an ex-convict and all, he just couldn't manage to get a lick o'work. People just wouldn't take him on."

Lowry took this one in his stride, even though it was an overpowering blow.

"An ex-convict, you say?"

"Sure, didn't you know?"

"I wasn't—a very close friend of his."

"Hey, you after him to collect some money from him, maybe?"

"No. Nothing like that. You see, one of Mack Wilson's friends is in very serious trouble, and Mack could be of some help if I could find him. What was he convicted of, do you know?"

"Did two years at San Quentin for robbery, that's what they said."

"I see," Lowry said weakly. "And you don't have any idea—"

"Afraid not."

"Okay," he said. "I guess that's all, then. Thanks a lot for your help."

"Thanks for nothing, mister."

The door slammed. Lowry walked away, his shoulders drooping in a defeated slump.

Chalk off one possibility for an avenue of defense.

It looked bad for McKay.

Very bad.

There were so few leads that could help him. And this one had fizzled completely and absolutely. Let alone the improbability of ever being able to locate any given migratory worker in as broad an area as Orange County, it would do hardly any good at all even if the man were to be found in time for trial. Hadn't the lawyer stressed the point that the witness for the defense would have to be absolutely reliable? What hope would there be for the acceptability of testimony from a witness who had served two years at San Quentin? He would be laughed off the stand, if Reynolds ever brought him up to testify, which Reynolds would never do. So he had to cross off the Mack Wilson avenue.

11

Depressed, Lowry drove back to his office. Phone calls and press releases had piled up in his absence, and he attended to them for a while, letting the routine and meaningless work take his mind off the sour feeling of defeat that oppressed him.

Finally, his desk clear, he began to write his column for the next day. The words flowed rapidly as his nimble fingers leaped over the keys of his ancient typewriter. When he had finished turning out the daily quota, he leaned back in the swivel chair and read the column through to see the feel of it. As he came to the last paragraph, he smiled with satisfaction. The last item he had written read as follows—

If you're on top in this town—and for all I know in every other town—make good and sure you stay there. And if you ever need a better reason for this sage bit of advice than just my say-so, I suggest you look through the papers of the past few days and learn a lesson from the experiences of Bob McKay.

Did any lad ever have more fair-weather friends than this one? And did any lad ever find himself more completely alone when the breaks turned bad for him? I know. Platitudes, everyone says when stuff such as this is gotten off. Everybody knows that the flies swarm around the sugar bowl and not the vinegar jar. I don't pretend to be a philosopher, but it seems to me that the case of Bob McKay is a sad and embittering commentary on our so-called civilization. If this is the way it is with human beings, will somebody please tell me what it's all worth?

Among the many thousands who read this bit was Terry Stafford, an ever-lovely Terry Stafford, but for the past few days a little pallid, a little tense and jumpy, torn between conflicting desires. A world, a whole phase of her life, had seemed to tumble down in fragments about her well-shaped head when she had first read in the newspapers that a seamy derelict named Bob McKay who had once been a personality in the entertainment world was charged with the brutal murder of a Main Street B-girl named Doris Blair.

Terry's first impulse had been to rush to the prison where McKay was being held, fall on her knees and weep with her lover for the miserable wreck they had made of their lives and of the love that once had been. But the mood passed quickly as she came to the realization that it wouldn't do any good whatsoever if she did go to McKay…even if she could somehow make herself forget that he had stubbornly refused to compromise a little, even for the sake of their mutual happiness…even if he would forget that she had been the one to cast him adrift as hopeless and beyond redemption because his strength, the drive that had put him where he was, seemed to have left him for good.

Visiting him could do him no good…poor, helpless Bob, she thought. And although she hated and despised herself for thinking it, she knew that the visit could do her a lot of harm. Why should she allow a thing that was better left in the discard heap, the battered and castoff love she had had for McKay once in the past, to stand between her and a driving ambition that alone might be able to serve as a substitute for what she had once wanted?

Jack Colin would put her across. She knew it for a fact. All she needed to do was to play her hand properly, and Colin would do anything she wanted him to do for her. He would build her up into the glittering star she craved to be. To allow her name to get mixed up in a sordid and brutal murder case at this stage would be to finish the career she wanted even before it had a chance to get started.

That was the way Terry Stafford reasoned. What couldn't be dealt with by reason became torture.

She smoked cigarette after cigarette and paced about her little apartment. Colin hadn't called in several days, and that had been worrying her. But now the telephone rang. Terry sprang to it.

It was Colin, at last.

He didn't say a word about the few days that had gone by in silence. But she detected an undercurrent in his tone that conveyed to her the fact that he was forgiving her for the callous way in which she had ignored his feelings the other night.

She hated him for his patronizing manner, and at the same time she wanted him to act quickly on her behalf, to start her along that gleaming road from which there would be no turning back, not ever, to the crushing heartbreak of the past.

"Are you free tonight?" he asked hopefully.

"I might be."

"What is that supposed to mean?"

"It's supposed to mean that I've got some tentative plans, but I could break them if something really important came up in a hurry."

"Do I rate as something really important, darling?" Colin asked.

She found the *darling* highly offensive. But it was necessary, she thought, just as the touch of Colin's lips on her lips was necessary, just as the grasping of his hands for the warm peaks of her bosom was necessary. Just as perhaps she might have to go to bed with him and endure his hands on her naked body and feel the pressure of his gross form above her, his weight on her, the sudden grunting as his animal lust satisfied itself—

It might all be necessary to get her to her goal. After that she could spit at the Jack Colins of the world. But first she had to reach the top.

"Yes," she said after some hesitation. "I'll get rid of my other arrangements. Come over tonight, yes, by all means."

"What's a good time?"

"Whenever's convenient, Jack."

"Let's make it seven, then. And I'll have dinner served. You won't have to do a thing."

The hours ticked away. Terry fidgeted about the small apartment, waiting for his arrival. The newspaper, which contained the impassioned column Lowry had written the day before, lay unopened on the table.

She did not dare to look through it now, yet she had been unable to keep herself from buying it. The compulsion to know what was happening to Bob had overwhelmed her at the newsstand, and she had quickly dropped her dime and snatched up the paper. Sooner or later she knew she would read what was in it.

She fought with herself to put off the moment. She told herself sternly that she must forget everything but Jack Colin, everything but what a man in Colin's exalted position could do for her. She forced herself to remember that she must never lose sight of what she wanted now. What she had left behind could only have led to ruin, could lead to ruin still.

Seven o'clock came.

Five after.

Ten after.

The doorbell rang. Terry, clad in a provocative low-cut dress, ran to answer it, her full breasts bobbing with every step she took.

"Jack!"

"Good evening, darling." Colin greeted her with his greasy smile, with an enormous cascade of flowers, and with a bottle of the very best Scotch. He set flowers and liquor down and held out his arms expectantly. Terry came to him, but the kiss that she gave him was a sisterly one, and she slid deftly away before he could turn the embrace into something more passionate. If he had noticed her coolness, he said nothing.

"You shouldn't have bothered with the flowers, Jack. They're lovely, but I'm always so sad when they wilt."

"You musn't be sentimental. Grasp beauty while it's here, and don't mourn when it fades."

"Is that the way you feel about women, too?"

He shrugged. "Could be. But a smart girl will prepare for the time when she isn't the sexiest thing on earth any longer. A bunch of roses can't invest in the stock market, you know." He laughed. "Mind if I use your phone? I want to get dinner up here."

He phoned down to a restaurant nearby, telling them it was time to deliver the meal, and an elaborate dinner, already prepared, was brought up to the apartment within a few minutes. A bowing headwaiter opened covered trays of sizzling rare steak and delectable vegetables, and before he left he opened a bottle of fine imported Burgundy to go with the meal. Colin tipped him handsomely, the size of the bill making Terry's eyes pop.

They ate and chatted, and Colin tried to be his witty best and almost succeeded, but that wasn't much. The wine gone, the dishes cleared away to be done some other time, they sat around and drank the Scotch he had brought. Terry suspected that Colin was hoping that the Scotch would react with the dinner wine to make her more susceptible to his advances, so she deliberately made her drinks weak and sipped them slowly.

Neither of them wanted to go out. It was cozy and warm in the apartment, and with the good dinner and the fine Scotch one could become expansive and loosen one's tongue to say what mattered. The problem that obsessed Terry was how she was going to overcome the unavoidable overtures he would make. She hoped for once that she would handle him successfully, regardless of what that might mean. She was resigned to surrendering herself to him ultimately, but then only once, after her career was assured.

12

Terry sat on the divan and Colin sat on the floor, bohemian fashion. Before settling down that way he had taken the precaution of drawing up his trousers at the knees, thus preserving the crease. Terry wondered how many years of wealth it took to make some men lose the habits they had cultivated in the days when pennies counted. Colin looked up at her, filling his eyes with adoration like a worshipful St. Bernard.

"You look a little tired, darling," he said in what he thought was a suavely sympathetic voice. "It can't detract from your loveliness, though. It makes you look like a Madonna."

"Really, Jack?"

"Really. But—you know something? I think I like you just a little less spiritual."

She forced a laugh. "I'll try, Jack," she said. "How would a handspring or two do to revive the spirit of youth in me?"

He smiled obscenely. His eyes twinkled. "I know some better ways."

"I'll bet you do."

"They involve two players."

"Count this one out."

"Why don't you want to play my games?"

"I guess I'm a spoilsport at heart."

He looked at her reproachfully. In a hurt, whining voice he said, "I don't understand. Is there anything wrong with me, Terry?" Was she really important to him to make him come down from the heights of his egotism that way, she wondered, or was this only a routine part of the act, a bit of business to bring into play when the more high-handed methods failed?

"Something wrong with you?" she said quietly. "Not that I know of, Jack."

He got up from the floor and sat down on the divan beside her. They were on dangerous ground once again, she knew.

"Then why do you give me the runaround this way?" he asked softly. "I've had a hell of a time over you, you know."

"I'm sorry, Jack."

"It doesn't have to be this way. It's like there's a wall between us. An invisible wall that I bang my head on every time I try to get near you."

She made no reply. He took her hand, then put his arm around her and drew her close to him. He kissed her, then hugged her tightly so that her chin rested on his shoulder. His hand stole up her side, coming to rest in its accustomed place over her breast, the fingers contracting nervously to tighten around the nipple. The other hand roamed down her back, over the tautness of her buttocks, then began to scoop under her dress and seek the waistband of her panties. He pressed hard against her to demonstrate the urgency of his desire, and she felt his heavy fingers against the skin of her belly, questing downward. Terry made no immediate attempt to resist him, even as his hand came to rest on her body, and his harsh breathing sounded in her ear as he prepared to fulfill his conquest of her. He was fumbling with her clothes, now, trying to undress her...

But as he held her, she looked out into space...across the room and to the picture on the table...and she remembered another time when a man had caressed her breasts, this time in love and not just in lust. The fair, boyish face smiled back at her from the picture, seemed to be laughing at her, and then it saddened right before her eyes.

She saw his face now looking worn and haggard, battered and bruised from beatings, with swellings along the jaw. She closed her eyes, but it was too late to shut out his image. He was walking hemmed in between two guards, a slow horrible walk such as Terry had seen in pictures, in the tabloids with somber captions underneath. He was walking to his death…to a meaningless death that nobody could explain.

She uttered a sharp cry.

Colin tensed in surprise. "What's the matter, Terry?" he asked anxiously.

Only then did she remember that she was still in the man's arms, that he had been caressing her body, trying to stimulate her into wanting to go to bed with him. The sickening realization that it was futile to try to live by her brain alone burst upon her with fierce savagery. She pushed Colin brusquely away from her and began to sob. Colin looked puzzled. "What—?"

"Leave me alone."

"What's wrong?" he demanded. "What's gone wrong this time?"

She shook her head, sobbing wordlessly.

The bewilderment in his face became anger. "Hell, Terry," he said, "I can't make you out at all. One minute you're a mature woman of the world, and the next you act like a silly high school girl out on a stupid necking party. What the devil's the matter with you, anyway? Will you tell me that?"

She stopped crying, the tears drying up as suddenly as they had begun.

"Go away, Jack. Please," she begged.

"Good God, Terry," he said in irritation. "Is it me or is there something wrong? Really wrong? Perhaps I could do something to help you."

"No, Jack. Just go away. I'll be all right. I just want to be alone."

He rose in a huff, shaking his head angrily. "And I thought you were one of the few real ones," he said. "That prima donna stuff doesn't impress me. I've seen too much of it. I'm not a schoolboy, you know. Hell, put on an 'I wanna be alone' act if that's what you want to do, but please don't think I've got nothing to do but wait around in between your moods."

She didn't answer him. He left without looking back at her.

She dried her eyes, then touched up her face with fresh makeup. Her eyes were large with grief but her mouth was drawn straight now in a firm determined line. She picked up the newspaper which she had been unable to touch earlier in the evening.

There was a news story, describing an interview with the District Attorney regarding the McKay case. Terry read quickly through it, but the story contained nothing that she hadn't already seen before.

She turned the pages rapidly, coming upon Lowry's column. His little sermon stared out at her from the bottom of the page. *I don't pretend to be a philosopher but it seems to me that the case of Bob McKay is a sad and embittering commentary on our so-called civilization. If this is the way it is with human beings, will somebody please tell me what it's all worth?*

Memories flew through her mind.

She sat at the table at the Lafayette, alone, watching while Bob McKay led his orchestra into the swing frenzies that made him famous. Everyone else was watching him, too, but she had that special feeling of knowing that he was playing not for them but for her. She saw Bob weaving around in circles as he blew his heart out on saxophone, trumpet, clarinet, anything that would respond to the dynamic, rhythmical power of his lungs.

And at the height of a number's wildness, at the peak of the bacchanalian ecstasy, he reeled around to face her and without taking his lips from the tightly held instrument he bared his teeth in a warm smile that told her he would be down as soon as he possibly could.

The fantastic music stopped abruptly.

The sudden silence in the big dance hall was practically deafening.

And then the hall burst into sound as the dancers and the listeners clamored noisily for more, unwilling to allow the warmth that had been stirred up in their blood to disappear, unwilling to let the savage emotions in their breasts subside back to everyday tranquility. Smiling, radiating back at them their own pleasure, McKay led the band into a slow waltz-time number. He was wringing wet with perspiration, his hair wild across his forehead. He quieted the nerves of the dancers, leading their thoughts into dreamier channels. The music became softer, died away altogether.

Then he was free for the intermission. He came down from the bandstand to sit by her side and took her hand, holding it in a way that expressed better than words his need for her. His big soft eyes were warm with his love and longing.

"You're exhausted, darling," she said sympathetically. "You refuse to spare yourself up there. It's too hard that way. You won't be able to keep it up. You'll burn yourself out."

"I've been doing it that way a long time," he replied with a shrug. "Can't switch now. I don't know any other music that's good. Not for me, anyway. This is my style and I'm stuck with it, like the color of my hair or my eyes or any other thing that can't be changed without making it look phony."

He mopped away the sweat, and then he turned and signaled to a waiter who was standing by, and the man nodded with instant understanding and headed for the bar, returning a moment or two later with a drink. She remembered the almost frightening eagerness with which he downed the drink that was brought him, the flash of fear that swept over her as she saw his consuming need for it, the way it calmed him, made him relax.

It had gone on like that for a long time.

It had become a lot worse.

Work till you drop.

Drink.

Work some more.

Drink some more.

"Work, work, work," he had said once to her. "Blow your heart out, your lungs, your brain. Never let up. It's the only way to live. You can't be half alive up there. But alcohol is a godsend for guys like me, Terry. Otherwise we'd never manage to stand the gaff, couldn't stick in the big money."

Well, he hadn't stood it anyway, even with the drinking. She should have known and told him they didn't need the big money, should have told him anything just to steady him and keep him from going off the rails. Terry hadn't done it. She had let him take that fast rocket to nowhere.

13

Now she felt that she was beginning to cry again. Angrily, she sniffed back the tears and poured herself a stiff drink. Bob had been right about drinking, in one way. It settled you down. But after a while the time came when you needed it and yet it still didn't help you any, and that was when you were finished.

She picked up a phone book and looked for the number of the *Gazette*. When she found it, she dialed the paper's office and asked for Lowry.

He picked up and said, "Lowry here."

"Hello. This is Terry Stafford," she said nervously. "Perhaps you remember me—"

"Of course I remember you, Terry," Lowry said. "It's part of my job never to forget a thing. Not that it would have been easy to forget you. It's awfully nice hearing from you. How has everything been?"

She ignored the unfortunate question.

"Could you come over here now, Ned? I'd like to talk to you. I think you can do me a lot of good."

At the other end of the wire, Lowry beamed. "I'll be over in a jiffy, Terry," he said. "Just tell me the address."

She gave it to him. She knew that he had understood what it was she wanted to see him about. That was why he hadn't even bothered to ask.

He was there in a jiffy, just as he had promised, smiling, hearty, unworried, unless you happened to look at him closely. If you did, you discovered that there was a restlessness in his eyes, a fidgety impatience that meant he was thinking about an innocent man who was cooped up behind bars.

"Tell me the truth, Ned," she said anxiously. "Is it really as bad for him as all the papers are saying? I mean—that they're certain to convict him—is it as bad as that—"

"Yes, Terry," he replied in a solemn voice. "It's rotten bad."

"Can't anything at all be done? Oh, Ned, isn't there any way at all—"

"I'm trying to dig up some evidence in his favor, Terry. But I can't say I've been having very much luck so far. I was down in El Centro today. I thought I might possibly find somebody who remembered having seen him down there."

"Did you?"

He shook his head dispiritedly. "I didn't. Not a soul. That's his alibi and there isn't a blessed thing with which he can support it. I talked with over a hundred truckmen who cover that route. What I had in my mind was that I might possibly find the man who had given him a lift. Normally I'd have stood a chance. It shouldn't be that hard to track down a witness or two. But as it is everything I try in this case seems to turn to ashes. It just seems as though it isn't meant that he should stand even the ghost of a chance. The cards are stacked against him."

Her thoughts ran riot. She clutched desperately at something.

"Must he stick to that alibi?"

"It's the truth."

"But if he can't prove the truth, couldn't he prove something else?"

"What do you mean?"

Color came to her face. She took a deep breath, and her breasts rose steeply. It was a moment before she said, "He could say that he spent the night with me. I'd swear to it right in court. I'd say he came here before midnight and stayed in bed with me until breakfast time. I don't give a damn what people will say about me, so long as what I do saves Bob's life."

Lowry took her hand in his. "You're a little nuts about the guy, aren't you, Terry?"

She smiled faintly. "I guess he's kind of hard to get out of your system."

Lowry shook his head. "It wouldn't do any good your saying a thing like that. Even if his story could be changed there's still the problem of the landlady who saw him leave the house at four in the morning."

"He could have left it to come here. That would still give him an alibi for the time of the murder."

"It isn't likely. It wouldn't hold water. They'd see you were going to bat for him, and there are plenty of girls who might be willing to lie away their reputations in court to save the life of the man they love—once loved. They'd feel sorry for you, not for him. But they wouldn't accept your testimony. No, it will have to be another way, if it's anything."

"If."

They sat down opposite each other, lit cigarettes, and groped feverishly for some valid idea. But ideas wouldn't come.

"They've been soft-pedalling Carrol himself," Terry remarked after a while. "That is, if I'm reading between the lines in the papers correctly."

"Very correctly," Lowry said. "Places like the kind Carrol runs can't do business without official sanction. First because they sell lousy liquor, second because of the girls they keep, third because they run a racing book. As a matter of fact, that place has an involvement in almost every angle that would make it necessary for Carrol to pay the cops off and for them to leave him be. Even so, the likelihood that Carrol killed the girl isn't very great."

"Why not?"

"Well, for one thing, Carrol's a lot too smart and a lot too hard to have gotten himself entangled with one of the girls who worked for him. Maybe he takes a grab at them now and then, but he doesn't get mixed up seriously with them. They were strictly business."

"But this one was supposed to be pretty, wasn't she? A lot more than most."

"Rather."

"Then mightn't he have forgotten his business principles just this one time?"

"What are you getting at, Terry?"

"I'm not sure I know. I'm just punching in the dark. What about the Filipino? Do you think maybe he did it?"

"Not a chance."

"Positive? He was on the spot."

"He's innocent and he's scared silly. That's how he happened to identify Bob, I'm sure. He's just anxious to say anything that'll take the spotlight off him, because he doesn't know what the hell this whole thing is all about."

Terry puffed rapidly at her cigarette. After another few moments of silence, during which she considered and rejected several wild ideas, she said, "You couldn't find out anything at Carrol's when you were there, could you, Ned. They know you too well at places like that."

"That's right. They shut up like clams when I come in."

"But I might hear something."

"You mean—"

"Exactly. I'm at least as attractive as the girls who work there, or don't you think so?"

"Much more." Lowry shook his head. "But it's a nasty job, baby. It's like swimming through a cesspool to spend an hour in a place like that. Do you think you'll make it?"

"I've got to," she answered evenly. "We can't let them execute Bob for a crime he didn't commit. Do you think Carrol will give me a job?"

"It's likely. You work on a percentage there, you know, so he has nothing to lose on your lack of experience." He tightened his jaws unhappily. "I don't like the idea, though. Are you sure you want to do it, Terry? It might become very unpleasant."

She shrugged. "Not any more so than it is right now. I'll mingle with the girls. They're bound to know something about Doris Blair. I've never heard of any woman who could remain a complete and absolute mystery to a group of women she saw every day."

Lowry nodded. "I thought of that slant. But of course there was no way I could get at them. They trust me about as much as they would the tax collector."

"I'll go to see Carrol tomorrow, then."

"Good luck, Terry. I hope you make it. Let me know how it's going."

"I will."

"Oh, and one thing you'd better remember. If I happen to walk into the place, you don't know me from Adam, of course. Otherwise we'll give the whole thing away and close up what may be our only remaining source of help."

"I understand."

Lowry stood up to go. As he walked to the door he stopped, turning around and smiling at the lovely girl. "It looks as if the crack I made in today's column doesn't go for you, Terry," he said. "I'm glad to know there are at least a couple of unselfish people left in this rotten world of ours."

In a quiet voice she said, "Your newspaper column applies to me as much as to anybody who ever knew Bob McKay. But they say that love is a selfish business. Otherwise I'd be stringing along with the others, I'll bet."

"I doubt it," he said with a casual grin. "So long, Terry. And watch out for yourself. Be careful."

14

Early the next evening, Terry put on a tight-fitting dress, very high-heeled shoes, and a heavy makeup which she felt gave her the requisite hard look. She folded a good evening gown into a tiny bag.

Boarding a downtown bus, she arrived at Carrol's half an hour later, and strode into the bar affecting the brisk, challenging manner she associated with the part she meant to play.

Only a few early drinkers sat at the bar, hunched over their drinks. The bartender, a sullen, bag-eyed fellow, swabbed down the counter and looked at her with chilly disdain.

"What's yours, Miss?"

She shook her head. "No, I'm not a customer. I'm—looking for Carrol."

"He expecting you?"

"No. But I'd like very much to see him."

The barkeep shrugged and nodded his head toward the back, without further explanation. Losing interest in her, he began polishing a chromium mixer with elaborate care.

Terry made her way toward the direction he had indicated. The place stank of stale beer. She went down a narrow corridor past the washrooms and came to a small room at the back with its door ajar.

Carrol was sitting near the window with his legs up on an ancient desk, reading a newspaper. He didn't put the paper down, just looked at her over the top of it. Terry experienced a shaky moment as she felt Carrol's heavy, penetrating eyes boring through the clinging dress she wore, running over her body from head to foot. She had a wild sensation of being stark naked in front of this man. His eyes seemed to strip away her clothing in order to rest lasciviously on the curves of her breasts and her tapering white thighs.

"Are you Mr. Carrol?" she asked nervously.

"Yeah," he said. His tone promised nothing and carried an implied suggestion that she had better get to the point in a hurry.

She moistened her lips.

"I'm looking for a job," she said simply.

Carrol shrugged. "There's an employment agency around the corner."

It was a rebuke, she felt, because she hadn't made her meaning clear enough.

"I meant a job here," she said nervously.

"Who told you we needed anybody?"

"No one. I've been going from door to door."

"Done this before?"

"No."

"There's a lot of angles, kiddo. I ain't running a goddam kindergarten here."

"I could manage it," she said quickly. "I can take care of myself." She walked up and back before him, chest inflated, breasts thrust out. He signaled for her to turn around, and she did. She felt ridiculous—but Carrol seemed to be impressed. He gave her another deep, searching look, and she felt queasy and dirty all over from the unblushing intimacy of the glance.

"It ain't bad," he said finally. "But the customers here don't know a good one from a bad. You gotta know how to talk to 'em."

"I've been talking a long time."

A faint smile broke through the crustiness of his face. But he wiped it off quickly.

"Got a dress?"

She held up the little bag in answer.

"Seven a week and a nickel on each drink they buy with you," he said. "That sound okay?"

"Y-yes."

"It damn well better, on account of that's all you're gonna get out of me," he said. "You stick around till closing, too. Any invites look good to you, you forget 'em. They spend whatever they spend right here, you understand? You walk off with some Johnny one night, just don't bother to come back. Everything okay?"

"I understand."

"Good. Put the dress on and you can go out."

She looked uncertainly around the room, waiting for him to show her where she could change. He said nothing, just looked expectantly at her. After a moment she said, "Will you tell me where the dressing room is?"

"There ain't none. The girls show up for work dressed. You put your clothes on right here."

"In front of you?"

"This ain't no job for a lady, kid," he said indifferently. "You change right here or you might as well scram the hell out of here."

Terry bit her lip. But there was no choice. If she didn't do as Carrol said, she would never accomplish what she had come here for. She hoped he didn't push her too hard...

Nervously she unzipped her skirt and stepped out of it. She was wearing a bra, panties, garter belt, and a half slip. Carrol eyed her with interest. She fumbled with the bag, taking the gown out. But just as she was about to put it on, Carrol drawled slowly, "Hold it, baby."

"What is it?"

He pointed to her straining bra. "Tell me are those goodies real or do you have cotton in there?"

Terry's face flamed. "I don't see where that's any of your business!"

"Listen," he said, his face growing ugly. "Everything that goes on around here is my business, get me? Including whether my girls wear falsies or not."

"You said yourself that the customers can't tell a good one from a bad—"

"Maybe *they* can't. But *I* can." He leered at her. "Kid, this town is full of girls who want to work in jobs like this. If you want to work here, you gotta be nice to me sometimes. I don't go for no insubordination. Take the bra off and let me have a look."

"And if I say no?"

"Then you can pack up and clear out."

Terry hesitated, her face crimson. She told herself that she would go this far, but no farther. If Carrol wanted her to strip completely, or to make love to her, she would refuse and try some other way of getting the information she wanted. There were limits...

She walked over and closed the door of the little room. Then, quickly, she unsnapped her bra. The cups fell from her breasts. A cool breeze travelled past her nipples.

She was conscious of Carrol's lustful gaze on her young flesh. The man was practically drooling. In her imagination, she saw him rising, coming toward her, ripping away her clothes. Saw him removing his clothes, forcing himself upon her. The idea of it all nearly sickened her. His gaze did not waver. She stood there, her face an icy mask, waiting for him to finish his disgusting inspection, praying that he would not want to handle and squeeze, as well as to see...

After perhaps thirty seconds he muttered, "Nice, baby. Damn nice."

She hooked the bra on again. Carrol was still smiling.

He seemed to be satisfied with a brief look, at least for now, because he made no further attempt to interfere with her as she hurriedly donned her evening gown. It was low-cut and daring, but what did that matter now that he had seen her bare breasts?

She fastened it. Carrol put the paper down and surveyed her again, moistening his thick lips and nodding approvingly.

"Nice rags," he said. "You was doin' all right for a while, huh?"

"It's been some time."

"I figured. Girls don't come here when they're making it good somewhere else."

"Can I go outside now?"

"Sure, baby. Get to work. Sit around and smile," he grunted. "The happier you make those boys, the more dough you'll walk out of here with. Take it slow. I'll be keeping an eye on you."

Terry sat at a table in one of the booths. There was a slight stir of early evening activity as working people on their way home dropped in for quick drinks. She felt self-conscious and ill at ease in the low-cut evening gown which made her look like a calendar illustration in that atmosphere. The girls began to arrive. They looked at her curiously but made no move to become acquainted. Three were blondes or near blondes, one was dark, one had red hair and strangely pale, blue eyes. She was older than the others and she had been drinking. Two men engaged the girls in loud, ribald conversation. They talked mild, suggestive smut. The girls laughed at the stale jokes—all but the red-haired one who seemed to have drunk only enough to make her morose and silent. She walked over to where Terry sat and gave her a tentative smile.

"Welcome to the menagerie," she said.

"Thank you," Terry said.

"Name's Lola, Lola Larsen."

"How do you do, Lola. I'm Terry. Terry Wade."

The other women saw them talking. They too came over, unable any longer to maintain the pose of indifference.

"Terry," Lola told them, pointing to Terry. She didn't bother to mention the names of the others.

"Been in town long?" one of the blondes asked.

"Quite some time, yes," Terry replied vaguely.

Customers began to drift in. Somebody put a nickel in the record machine and a crooner began to wail about a hopeless love. The evening wore on.

The bar was crowded and Terry sat between two middle-aged men who had come in drunk. They tasted the drinks they had ordered, then left them on the bar and vied with each other for her attention. She listened to details about their personal tastes in women, growing apprehensive as she found that she did not know how to make them drink and buy more drinks. She finished the glass of Scotch that stood before her and asked if she could have another. They ordered it, then argued with each other about the privilege of paying. They left their own glasses almost untouched.

15

The room became filled with smoke, the smell of men who did not bathe too often and the cheap perfume the girls used. The record machine played constantly now. The two men finished their drinks and ordered more which they ignored just as they had done before. She had to quit after her third Scotch. The thought of drinking any more sickened her. The men began to notice that her monosyllabic replies to their questions were mechanical, that she was not listening to them.

"This place reminds me of a damn funeral parlor," one told the other.

"'S a fact," his friend said. "Le's get the hell out'a here."

They departed and Terry sat alone. The crowd began to thin out. Two of the girls—a blonde and the one called Lola—were sitting alone now, too. Lola came over and sat down next to Terry. She was drunk.

"How ya' doin', honey?" she asked.

Terry shrugged.

"Maybe ya' got no sex appeal, huh?" Lola laughed raucously.

"Maybe."

Carrol came over and stood behind them. Lola turned a smile on him.

"Slow night, Buck," she said.

"Yeah," he said sourly.

"Business ain't so good," she said sympathetically.

He looked around the room. Some of the stools at the bar were unoccupied now. The record music seemed to echo through the place. Carrol moved off.

"Nice feller when you get to know him," Lola said.

"Do you know him?" Terry asked.

"I ought to. I've been here a long time. He leaves people alone. I like that, don't you?"

"Yes."

"Good feller, too," Lola went on. Her tone was maudlin now. "Helps people out without advertisin' it."

"That's sweet."

"You said it. We had a kid here, came in half starved. Didn't have a dime. He put her on her feet. Didn't ask for anything. Think he got any gratitude? No, first thing you know she was actin' like Queen of the May. Started tearin' around."

"Yes?" Terry could not suppress her eagerness.

"Yeah," Lola said bitterly. "She wound up in the morgue," she added with satisfaction. "Too smart, that's what she was."

"How awful! Did she have an accident?"

"You said it. And she was gonna be a big shot. I told her she'd get the short end of the stick sooner or later. She did, too."

"Men," Terry sighed tragically.

"Yeah, men."

"I read about it. They found the man who killed her, didn't they?"

"Looks like it," Lola chuckled. "Who'd ever ha' thought that sucker'd be called Buzzy?"

Terry's glance sharpened. This was something important for sure.

"Buzzy?" she repeated.

"Sure. She used to tell me Buzzy'd give her half the world on a golden platter one of these days. And then this gold-plated Buzzy of hers turns out to be nothing but a bum. A stinking wino."

"She talked about him, did she?" Terry asked, leaning forward with interest.

"Yeah, but you'd a thought he had something, she was so goddam mysterious about it. And then what is he? Just a bum, that's who Buzzy was."

"You mean the man they pinched?"

Lola nodded her head solemnly. She seemed to be too drunk to realize that Terry was pumping her for information. But as Terry searched for the next question to ask, without wanting to seem obvious about it, the conversation was interrupted.

Carrol appeared. He stood in the doorway leading to the rear, looking at her. She tried not to meet his glance. But eventually she had to. He caught her eye and signaled to her to leave the bar. Then he went inside without a word.

Lola giggled. "Looks like the boss wants you, huh, kid?"

"Looks that way," Terry said tightly.

"Give him a good time," Lola said with a leer. "That's what he likes. A real good time."

"I'll bet," Terry said. "Excuse me."

She got up and crossed the room, heading in the direction Carrol had gone. He was waiting for her in the back room. He looked mean.

"What the hell you think you're doin'?" he demanded blusteringly. "Just sitting around on your can gassin' with that dame."

Terry shrugged. "There doesn't seem to be anything for me to do right at this particular minute," she said cautiously.

Carrol sneered and said, "There won't be, either, the way you're goin' about it. Hell, I thought you said you could manage it."

"Did I?" she asked archly.

Carrol got slowly to his feet. He was a big man, with a big

man's slowness, but Terry got the idea that he could move fast if he ever had to.

He was nodding. "Yeah, it is pretty slow out there," he said quietly.

She felt his eyes boring lustfully through her clothes again. She said nothing.

Carrol smiled. "Maybe you're wastin' your time anyway," he said.

"What do you mean by that?"

"Maybe you can do better for yourself than just trying to work the stews out there. You've got class, you know that? You could be doing a lot better for yourself some other way."

"For instance?"

"Shacking with me," he said bluntly.

Terry glared at him. "You've got big ideas, huh?"

"I'm a fussy guy," Carrol said. "But I like you, Terry. I could help you go places. Come here, will you? You stand over there like I got leprosy or something, you know that?"

She shrank back nervously. He crossed the room in a couple of big strides and came close to her, extending his big paws and dragging her to him. One hand closed on her breast, squeezing it painfully through the fabric of her gown. She heard his harsh breathing, felt his big fingers trying to work their way through the fabric to the warm flesh beneath. She struggled to get away from him and finally succeeded. She stepped back, breathing hard.

"I didn't bargain for that," she snapped. "I don't like to be pawed."

He looked hurt. "Aw, don't be so sensitive," he crooned. "I ain't hard to take. You'll do all right with me, Terry."

He reached out for her again, pulling her roughly toward him. Again the big hand groped for her breasts. She felt the thick fingers probing down through her neckline. His lips were against hers. She wedged her hands against his shoulders and tried to push him away, but it was like trying to push a mountain.

He was trying to get his hand between her breasts. When he came up for air from the kiss, he was panting harshly, like some bestial creature.

Suddenly the door opened behind them. Carrol released her instantly. Terry saw Lola standing in the doorway, veering drunkenly from side to side.

"Don't be a louse, Buck," Lola said in a wobbly voice. "Maybe the kid don't want to play games with you. You ever figure on that?"

Carrol was furious. "Who the hell said you could come bustin' in here?" he growled.

"I wanted to talk to you. I got something important to say to you."

"How many times I told you never open that door when it's shut?" Carrol stormed.

Lola was too drunk to care. "I wanted to talk to you."

"Later."

"Leave the poor kid alone."

"Christ!" Carrol bellowed. He threw up his hands. "Who you think you are, telling me what I can do and what I can't?"

16

Terry didn't wait around to see what would happen. She slipped past Carrol, through the open door.

She found her bag in the hall where she had left it. She picked it up and hurried out, through the front of the saloon. The girls looked at her in astonishment as she rushed quickly past them.

"Hey, Bright Eyes!" the dark one snickered derisively. "How come you're quitting so soon?"

Terry didn't bother to answer. There was a cab on the corner. Terry gave the driver her address. She opened the window and the cool air rushed in, calming her a little. Still she sat on the edge of the seat, thinking frantically.

When she returned to her apartment, the first thing she did was to telephone the office of the *Gazette* and ask for Lowry. It took a couple of minutes till they found him. Finally he picked up the phone.

"Lowry speaking."

"I'm home," she told him simply.

"Terry?"

"Who else?"

"Quickest job you ever had, I'll bet," he said. "What happened?"

"You'd better come over, I think. I'll tell you all the gory details when you're here. We'll have to puzzle it out."

"I'm finishing up some stuff," he said.

"How soon will you be through?"

"Soon as I can make it. I'll hustle right over," he said and hung up.

While she waited she changed her clothes again, getting out of the gown and into something less dressy, a polo shirt and a pair of black toreador pants. Then she settled down impatiently to wait for Lowry's arrival. Less than an hour went by, and then there was a knock at the door.

"You finished up your work fast enough," she said as she opened the door.

Then she gasped.

It wasn't Lowry.

It was Carrol.

He stood in the doorway, big and menacing-looking. She started to shut the door on him, an automatic reflex. But he grabbed it and pushed it open again. He shouldered his way past her into the apartment and closed the door behind him.

"You ain't the only one who moves fast, sister," he said with an ugly grin.

"How did you get here? What do you want?" The questions tumbled off Terry's lips.

"The cabbie was back at his stand in no time, if you really have to know. He didn't mind another long fare. Sit down and relax," Carrol invited.

"What do you want?" Terry repeated.

"I want to know what you wanted. Sit down, I said." It wasn't an invitation this time, it was a blunt command. Frightened, Terry backed up until she reached the high-backed chair, and she sat down in it. He plumped down on the divan and calmly lit a cigarette. His gaze rested on the fabric of her tight polo shirt, taut against the interesting contours of her breasts.

He said, "I almost spotted you—but not quite. Who sent you?"

"I don't know what on earth you're talking about," Terry said.

Carrol slid forward to the edge of the divan. The glint in his eyes told the girl that he would very likely be interested in finishing his interrupted attempt at raping her. She shuddered in disgust at the idea of any kind of intimate contact with this man.

He said, "We won't get any place that way. From what I heard, you had trouble on your mind. I don't like trouble, do you understand?"

"Please leave me alone."

"I said I don't like trouble. Now, what's up? If you want to know something, why don't you ask me? Maybe I can tell you."

She said nothing. His glance slowly moved up her body and then wandered away, coming to rest on the framed photograph of McKay. His face grew hard.

"That's what I thought," he said. "Sister, the next time you want to pump somebody, don't pump a stewed dame. They talk all over the place."

"I want you to leave me alone."

"I'm not through yet. You—"

There was a sound outside the door. Carrol went suddenly tense and looked from the door to her. Terry didn't move. There was a knock.

"Open it," Carrol said in a low tone.

She went to the door. It was Lowry. A glance at his face and Terry knew he had overheard something of what had just passed between her and Carrol.

Lowry came inside. Carrol got up, scowling at both of them.

"Kid Seamy Side himself," Carrol said. "Quite a coincidence, huh, Lowry?"

"Aren't you on the wrong side of town right now, Carrol?" Lowry asked sourly. "Not that I want to sound snobbish."

"Not that you want to sound off any which way, Lowry," Carrol said menacingly. "I don't like this business."

"What business?"

"No double-talk," Carrol snapped. "My place is well out of this McKay rap, do you get me straight? I don't want no halfwits with ideas out of movie shows lousing things up for me."

"You interest me, Carrol," Lowry said airily. "I presume you followed Miss Stafford all the way out here just to tell her that. You must be real worried to do a thing like that."

"Yes," Terry put in. "I think Buzzy is worried."

"Buzzy?" Lowry asked curiously.

Carrol's face was a cold mask. "What kind of gag is that?" he asked through his teeth.

"You are Buzzy, aren't you, Mr. Carrol?" Terry asked innocently.

Carrol took a quick step toward her. "Look, bimbo, something's on your mind that ain't gonna do you no good at all. If you think you know something I don't know, speak up or else—" He raised his hand as if to strike her.

"I think the lady informed me that she was no longer in your employ, Carrol," Lowry said in a dry, tight voice. "That in itself seems reason enough why you shouldn't have the privilege of socking her." He moved nearer to Carrol. "To say nothing of the fact that she's a friend of mine and you're forgetting your manners."

Lowry emphasized his reprimand with a well-aimed right that caught Carrol flush on the jaw and sent him to the floor. He lay there stunned for a moment, then reached for his coat pocket.

"Ned!" Terry screamed.

But Lowry saw the gesture. He kicked Carrol's hand sharply. Carrol gasped with pain as his hand remained suspended lifeless in mid-air. Lowry bent over and yanked Carrol up by the collar. He hustled him over to the door and turned his head to Terry.

"I was right, wasn't I, Miss Stafford, in assuming that the gentleman was not a welcome caller?"

"You were right," Terry said.

Lowry opened the door and pushed Carrol out with a hearty shove that sent him banging against the wall opposite the door. Then he closed the door and bolted it.

"Now," he said to Terry. "All we have to do is open a window for some fresh air, and it'll be as if he was never here."

"Never mind the window, Ned," she said excitedly. "Do you think we ought to let him get away?"

Lowry chuckled. "You don't really want him around, do you?"

"No, of course not, silly. But he's the man, Ned, can't you see?

"I found out from one of the girls," she added quickly. "There was a man Doris Blair called Buzzy. He was doing things for her in style or was going to. That must be Carrol. The man's a chaser. His indifference to feminine charm is a pose."

"What makes you so sure of that, Terry?" Lowry asked provocatively.

"I blundered into a room with him. I ought to know."

"You may be right, but you're drawing the wrong conclusion if it's because Carrol made a pass at you. An anchorite would do that."

"Ned, this is serious. Doris Blair worked for Carrol. That girl who told me about it said he had taken her in when she was starving. Who else would a girl meet in that environment who could do things for her? And who else would think of strangling her when she got to be too much of a nuisance?"

"Sounds good, Terry. What do you suggest?"

"Let's go to the police."

Lowry shook his head. "With what except our suspicions? Do we know for a fact that Carrol kept the girl? Is there any evidence? Do you suppose the police would be interested in that kind of suspect when they've already got a man who's been identified? It will take more than that before we can go to them." He looked at his watch. "It's late but the landlady might not throw more than a broom or two at us. Suppose we hop over to the place where Doris lived. We might find something that will shed some light."

"Do you know where she lived?"

"I've found out that much," he said ruefully.

17

Lowry had his car outside. They drove downtown and stopped in a neighborhood of cheap hotels. Among them was a three-story brick building with a sign outside that read, "Rooms and Housekeeping Rooms." Lowry and Terry went inside. It was musty and dingy and smelled of bad cooking. Lowry knocked at the door of an apartment marked "Manager." A short stout woman came to the door.

"We got no more vacancies," she said before Lowry could speak, "and anyway we don't show rooms this time of the night."

"Glad to know business is so good," Lowry said. "But we weren't looking for a vacancy. I'm Ned Lowry from the *Gazette*."

"Listen, Mister," the woman said. "I've had a bellyful of you reporters in the last few weeks. I've got nothin' more to tell you about that Blair girl than you've had in the papers already."

"Still, if you don't mind," Lowry persisted ingratiatingly. "Just a few questions and could we see her apartment. It's an assignment I must fill or the boss'll fire me. He swore he would."

The woman looked at Terry. "What'd you need her along for if you're that busy," she asked Lowry suspiciously.

"Couldn't leave her alone. She's afraid to be alone."

"Oh, your wife, huh?"

"Yeah," Lowry grinned. "My wife."

"All right, what do you want to know?"

"The phone is in the hall here, I suppose."

"That's right."

"Did you ever hear Doris Blair talk to a man on the phone whom she called Buzzy?"

"Once or twice but don't get the idea I've got nothin' to do but listen in on tenants' conversations."

"Of course not. He called her on those occasions, I imagine."

"Sure, I called her to the phone myself. It didn't happen more than two or three times."

"What did he sound like?"

"Had kind of a smooth voice. The cops said that checked perfectly with this feller McKay they got."

"Everything seems to have done that," Lowry muttered. "You never saw him come here, did you?"

The woman drew herself up to her full height. "I should say not, mister. This is a respectable house. You don't catch nothin' like that goin' on here."

"I didn't mean that, of course," Lowry said quickly. "When was the last time he called?"

"Couple of weeks ago. She didn't turn up for two days after that."

Lowry's ears perked up. "Do you remember what day it was?"

"Yes, it was a Friday. I'm pretty sure."

"Good for you, my good woman, and thank you. Now could you let us have a look at the apartment she lived in?"

"It's rented. The people have been in there a couple of days now. But it wouldn't have made any difference. The cops took everything the girl had out of there."

"I see. Well, thanks again."

"Forget it. But don't come bustin' in at this hour again for news stories or I won't care if they do fire you."

When they were outside again, Terry said. "Well, what do we know now that we didn't know before?"

"We know that Buzzy called her on a Friday for the last time."

"Which means what?"

"I don't know yet," Lowry said slowly, "but it may be important later. I have an idea there's something wrong with the way we've been going about this. I guess it's lucky I have a job. I'd never make a detective."

"What's wrong?"

"Well, I think we ought to go back as far as we can, working on whatever happened to anybody involved, in chronological order. Things might follow through then. For instance, there's that Filipino, Ramirez. He was the first one to know about the murder. Maybe he can help us. I think I'll go see him."

"Let's go."

"I said I'll go see him. You're going home first," Lowry said.

"Please, Ned. Stop treating me as though I'm ninety years old. I want to go with you. I wouldn't be able to sleep anyway."

But he was adamant. Having the girl along would only make it harder to deal with the already frightened and suspicious Ramirez.

"Sorry, lady. It's too late for you to be making calls on strange men."

"But—"

"No."

Lowry drove rapidly back to Hollywood and saw Terry safely into the apartment.

"If Carrol comes back, slug him," Lowry told her. "But I don't think he'll be back here tonight. He'll be needing a rest."

He drove back downtown. Ramirez' shack was at the edge of a lot that had somehow escaped being used as an industrial site. It was only a short distance from a maze of factories, railroad sidings, and warehouses.

At that hour the neighborhood was as quiet and deserted as the remotest cabin of some early pioneer. Lowry walked up to the ramshackle shack and knocked briskly at the door. Through the window, he saw somebody lighting an oil lamp.

A moment later, the Filipino opened the door a trifle and looked up at Lowry through frightened, sleepy eyes.

Lowry smiled pleasantly.

"It's little late to come calling, I know," he said. "But I hope you won't mind. It's fairly important. I'm Ned Lowry from the *Gazette*. Do you mind if I come in and talk to you?"

The Filipino hesitated. For an instant Lowry thought that he was going simply to close the door on him and go back to sleep.

"It's all right," Lowry said persuasively. "I just wanted to talk to you about McKay."

He was sorry he said it, almost instantly. Ramirez began to tremble, and his thin, drawn face grew pale and tense.

"Please. No talking. I have to work in the morning," he said agitatedly. "I must go back to sleep. We talk some other time."

Lowry grew impatient. "I won't hurt you," he said. "I'm just here to talk to you, not to get you into trouble."

He pushed the door open and went past Ramirez into the small room. The place was furnished with a weird assortment of miserable, cast-off odds and ends of chairs and tables. Behind a drawn curtain, frayed and moth-holed, Lowry saw a mattress and blanket on the floor, without linens.

He sat down on a rickety chair and offered Ramirez a cigarette. The Filipino shook his head nervously. Lowry lit one himself.

The Filipino broke the silence. "What do you want from me?" he quavered.

"Some information."

"About what? I know nothing."

"Why did you say McKay killed that girl?" Lowry demanded harshly.

"I see him."

"Like hell you did," Lowry blazed. "How could you see him in the dark?"

Ramirez' eyes shifted uneasily. He looked very terrified. "It was not dark. It was almost light. I see him then."

Lowry got up and waved the Filipino to his feet.

"Come on. Show me where you saw him."

"What you mean?"

Lowry scowled. "Put a coat on and come on outside and show me where you saw him."

Trembling, afraid to speak, the terror-stricken Ramirez drew a heavy, dirty sweater around his shoulders and opened the door.

"This way," he grunted.

Lowry followed him at least fifty feet from the cabin to a patch of high woods.

"Here," Ramirez said.

Lowry looked back to the house and said, "And from that distance you saw the man so that you could identify him?"

"Yes."

Lowry muttered a curse and started back to the house. Ramirez followed him with short, quick steps. Lowry sat down again.

He stared at the Filipino. "You were afraid, weren't you, Ramirez?" he said. "You can tell me. I'm not a policeman. You were afraid they would accuse you of the murder, weren't you?"

Ramirez shook his head violently. "No, I did not do it."

Speaking with care, Lowry said, "I didn't say you did it. I said you were afraid that they would accuse you, so you said it was McKay."

The little man looked up sullenly. "He look like the man I see," he said weakly.

"He looked like him. Sure. But a lot of men could have looked like him. You didn't see him clearly, Ramirez. You could even have said I looked like him, if you had seen me in the lineup, couldn't you?"

"No, you are too big."

Seeing he was getting no place fast, Lowry steered a different course.

"Look, Ramirez, do you know what you have done? Unless a miracle happens, an innocent man is going to die before very long because you were afraid they would accuse you of something that they could never ever prove you did."

The Filipino began to look genuinely alarmed. "What you mean?"

"They frightened you down at the police station. They could never have proved you were guilty. There was no evidence, no motive. Do you understand what I'm trying to tell you?"

18

The door opened suddenly and Brady stood framed in the dim light in the doorway. He looked from Lowry to Ramirez and his jaw jutted out considerably farther than usual.

"You don't understand what he's talking about, Ramirez, because he's lying to you," he said. He turned angrily toward Lowry. "You're getting around a lot tonight, aren't you, Mr. Lonelyhearts?"

Lowry glared right back. He was far beyond the pretense of pleasantness.

"And you seem to be doing a very effective job of tailing me, Brady."

"Maybe so."

"It's too bad, you know. I'm not a criminal, friend. You'd have lost me long ago if I were."

"Don't be so sure about that, Lowry. And what's more. I'm not so sure you're all as pure and simple as you claim."

"No?"

"What's McKay know that's got you so worried, will you tell me that?"

"Meaning what?"

"Meaning the way you're tearing around the whole goddam county, trying to get him out of the clink and him guilty as hell. I'm not so sure you ain't afraid he won't spill a little piece about you."

"Your imagination is improving by leaps and bounds, Brady. This new wrinkle is a really downright interesting idea."

"I think so, too. You knew the Blair dame. She was a hot

number. Could've given even a guy like you a lot of trouble, Lowry."

"Really?"

"I was thinking maybe she had something you thought you'd better get your hands on before we did. That's why you were smellin' around the dump she lived in tonight, Lowry."

"Brilliant deduction, Brady. I'll give you the Sherlock Holmes Medal of Honor for that. And maybe you can explain why I took Terry Stafford with me."

"Why not? The Stafford girl was the best cover you could think of."

Lowry got up. "You know you're talking a stream of rubbish, Brady, and you know why." He pointed to the silent, large-eyed Ramirez. "You've got this poor guy here scared out of his wits, and you aim to keep him that way. Unless he sticks to his story, no jury in the state would convict McKay. Do you know where he saw this murderer?" Lowry went to the window and waved his hand in the direction of the darkness outside. "At a distance of over fifty feet in little better than complete darkness. You're going to look very foolish when this is over, Brady."

Brady's face was red with anger. "And you're going to look a damned sight worse than that in a minute or two, Lowry, if you don't get your nosy butt right out of here pronto."

Lowry smiled levelly. "I thought that was what was worrying you. Well, I'm going, Brady. You have the rest of the night to browbeat this helpless chap. Make sure you do a good job."

He started for the door, then turned to Ramirez and said quietly, "So long, Ramirez. And don't worry. It won't hurt you to tell the truth."

Lowry got into his car and drove rapidly off. Back in his apartment, he poured himself a good stiff shot of rye and sat

down to think over what had just happened and what, if anything, he had learned.

The phone rang. It was Terry.

"What are you doing up so late?" he asked.

"I had to call you," she said urgently. "Did you learn anything?"

"Nothing definite," he said. "But I'm sure now that Ramirez
identified McKay only because he was just too frightened to do
anything else. Brady thrives on bulldozing people. Well, I got
in a few licks with Ramirez that will set him thinking. Even if I
find nothing else I don't think the trial will be a pushover. A
decent lawyer ought to be able to punch that Filipino's story
full of holes."

"What do we do next, Ned?"

Lowry paused. "Well, I guess the next thing we have to do
is account for the identity of this Buzzy. I'll look around tomorrow."

"Let me know if you think I can help."

"Will do."

"I haven't done much good so far, I'm afraid," Terry said.

"On the contrary," Lowry assured her. "If that name Buzzy
means anything, you've done plenty, Terry. Plenty."

Lowry was in Reynolds' office early the following morning. He
recounted the events of the night before, the lawyer listening
carefully and taking an occasional note on his scratch pad.

When Lowry was through, Reynolds said, "That's it, huh?"

"That's it."

"Well, it'll be a good idea to break down Ramirez that way,"
Reynolds said. "All they have are these two witnesses, Ramirez
and Dr. Clayton. McKay's landlady's evidence that she saw him
leave the house at four in the morning is merely circumstantial."

"It's a hell of a way for things to be," Lowry said sadly. "To pull a fellow in, brand him guilty and then let his friends prove that he isn't if they can."

"This isn't exactly a Utopia we're living in, if that's what you mean to say," Reynolds remarked drily. "You could try Clayton now. Find out how sure he was that it was McKay. Maybe you could plant some seeds of doubt there. If we can shovel dirt on both of the key witnesses, it'll mean a lot for McKay."

Lowry nodded. "Right. I'll head straight out to see Clayton now."

19

In the spruce, well-kept and exclusive Westwood district, Lowry found Clayton's home. It was a big, comfortable-looking house, sparkling with white freshness and surrounded by giant palms and spacious flower gardens.

Dr. Clayton was still having his morning office hours, a trim nurse with a fixed professional smile informed Lowry.

"Would you care to wait for him?" she asked.

"All right."

"You're a new patient, aren't you?"

"No, I'm not a patient at all. I'm here to see the doctor about a personal matter."

"Very well, then."

The only other occupant of the waiting room was an overfed, overdressed woman who kept moving impatiently from one chair to another. Lowry saw her prepare to speak and then she looked brightly at him.

"Don't you think Dr. Clayton is a wonderful doctor?" she asked confidentially.

"An excellent doctor," Lowry agreed.

She grinned delightedly. "All my friends say so, too. He's done wonders for me. Of course," she added in a lower tone, "he is a little high, but I think it's worth it."

"I'm sure it is."

The door opened and the nurse called the woman in. It was fifteen minutes before she came out and then the nurse told Lowry Dr. Clayton would see him.

Clayton's inner sanctum was in keeping with the rest of the house and the impression it gave of solid comfort bordered on luxury. Clayton himself, sitting behind a massive desk was a handsome, capable-looking man. He greeted Lowry pleasantly and if he didn't show any real warmth when Lowry told him who he was, he was mildly cordial.

"There's no reason, Dr. Clayton," Lowry said, "for this McKay affair to really concern you. You did, I am sure, what you thought was your duty in identifying him and I've no doubt you were quite certain you had identified the right man. However, I and one or two other of McKay's friends are quite convinced of his innocence and we are sure some terrible mistakes have been made. Of course, to the police, it is a closed case. They've got their man so far as they're concerned. But we feel there must be some things that have been overlooked, some little thing that might serve to prove he could not have been guilty."

"It's unfortunate," Clayton said thoughtfully. "As you say, I did what I thought was right in identifying McKay but I'd rather not have done so at all. I will say that he definitely looks like the man who held me up but as I tried to tell the police no man can be absolutely sure considering the circumstances. Still they insisted that if he looked like the man it was my business to say so."

"But do you realize that your testimony will be his death warrant?"

"It couldn't be only that. Somebody else identified him. You're his friend, Mr. Lowry. It doesn't seem possible to you that he could have done it but those things just happen."

"Then you believe it was McKay."

"I think it was."

"Would you mind if I checked over the events of that night with you? There may be something that would shed some light. I won't take much of your time."

"Of course not. If there's any possibility that it wasn't McKay, I'd be glad if I could help you prove it."

"You were called down to a patient that morning and you drove down and left your car outside the house."

"Yes, a charity case I encountered in the clinic, a child who gets some pretty violent asthmatic attacks."

"When you came out of the patient's house, the man you think was McKay was in the back of your car and held you up at the point of a gun."

"That's right. He took my wallet, removed the bills and flung the rest back at me, then he made me turn over the car keys to him and forced me out."

"Wasn't it quite dark?"

"Yes but there was a street lamp a little way off."

"And that shed enough light so that you could see this man?"

"As well as I said I saw him. Now, don't misunderstand. I insisted and I still insist that I cannot be sure it was McKay. I can only say that it looked like him. I don't think the man who held me up was speaking in a natural tone of voice so that's nothing to go by. I don't intend at any time to say that I know it was McKay, now or at the trial, but if MacKay looks like the man and they find corroborating evidence to prove his guilt, I can't help feeling that I've done the right thing. Or, if I did think McKay looked like the man, would you have me say flatly that I was certain he looked nothing like him?"

Lowry got up. "No, Dr. Clayton. I suppose you did what you thought was best. It's just made it awfully tough for McKay. Now, would there have been any likelihood that the people in the home of your patient had seen somebody prowling around the place?"

"I don't know. They never mentioned it."

"Would you mind giving me the address. I'd like to talk to them and make certain."

"Not at all."

Clayton pressed a button on the desk and the nurse came in.

"Give Mr. Lowry the Lawrence girl's address," he told her. "If there's anything else I can do," he said to Lowry, "I'll be glad to. If you're right about your friend's innocence I hope you can prove it."

"I suppose the police currycombed the car," Lowry said.

"I imagine so. At least there was nothing in it after it was returned to me."

"Well, thank you, Dr. Clayton."

"Not at all," Clayton said. He walked with Lowry to the door. Outside, the nurse produced a little card from a file she kept on the corner of her desk, and she read off the name and address to Lowry, who scribbled it down in his notebook.

There was another patient in the room, now, a man of about forty, well dressed, prosperous looking, secure, Lowry thought, in the comforting knowledge that here he would be getting the very best medical attention that money could buy.

Everything was like that about the office and the house as well—solid on a foundation of money, competence. Lowry looked at the address he had just taken down and went out across the broad verandah, which he took in more appreciatively now that the interview with Clayton was behind him.

In the garden, a good-looking woman in a light tan slack suit and a pretty little girl with long, braided blonde hair were standing deep in a small patch of vivid crimson poinsettias. As Lowry went down the stairs the child turned to look at him. She was blue eyed, tiny featured, an exquisite child. She smiled warmly at Lowry and he stopped to admire the lovely picture she made, standing there, tiny and fragile amidst the tall plants.

20

"Would you like one?" the child asked simply in a sweet voice.

"I'd love to have one," Lowry said.

The woman turned around to look at him carefully. She had a long, austere, thin-lipped face, attractive in a remote way but cold. And Lowry thought there was a sadness in the eyes which perhaps she was disguising with the coldness.

"Lovely day," Lowry said.

"Isn't it?" she replied with frosty but automatic politeness.

The little girl was coming toward him bearing a huge poinsettia. The woman watched her, seeming neither to approve nor to disapprove.

The child handed Lowry the flower.

"It is a lovely day, isn't it?" she said softly, parrotlike.

Lowry took the flower and bowed low in front of the child. "Thank you most kindly, Miss," he said graciously. "And you're absolutely right. It is a lovely day."

The little girl smiled brightly, showing pearly baby teeth. "I wish I was at the beach when the sun shines like this," she said. "Then I could dig in the sand."

"What would you dig for?"

"Oh, I don't know," she replied without a trace of embarrassment or self-consciousness. "But there's treasure in the sand, they say. Maybe I might find some treasure if I had good luck."

"Well, then I hope you can go to the beach and find a wonderful treasure very soon."

"Oh, I'll be going before long," the child said happily. "Mother says we can go to the house in Laguna just as soon as the weather gets a little bit warmer." She turned to the woman for confirmation. "Didn't you say that, mother?"

"Yes, dear," her mother said. "But say goodbye to the nice man, now. You'd better come back and help me finish with the garden. It's almost time for you to have your lunch."

"My name is Lorna Clayton," the child said pleasantly, as she started to climb back into the flower bed. "What's yours?"

"Ned Lowry," Lowry said. He grinned broadly at the pretty little child. "See you again sometime, Lorna. And thanks for the flowers."

She waved a white, dainty hand to him as he swung down the walk toward his car. Her mother was bending over the plants again.

Lowry got into the car, frowning thoughtfully. The visit to Clayton had not been very fruitful, but perhaps some unexpected good would come out of an avenue he did not fully appreciate now. It was worth keeping in mind, at any rate. With so little to go on, every scrap of information was precious.

He drove downtown and quickly found the address that the nurse had given him. The place was less than a quarter of a mile from Ramirez' shack and the empty lot.

It was dismal. The house was slate gray, a wooden shack, sooty and decrepit and dingy, exuding the sour stink of grinding poverty. Lowry looked up and down the street, estimating. Clayton's car would have been parked there, about thirty feet from the lamp post.

He knocked at the door.

After a long pause, a young woman opened the door. She was a pretty woman, but with the ordinary prettiness of the country girl. Her face was badly made up with cheap rouge and her hair was dry and brittle. She wore a coarse linen blouse. Her breasts were big and full, almost abnormally so, leading

Lowry to conclude that she was either astonishingly well developed or else nursing a child. More likely the latter, he thought.

Lowry went through the process of introducing himself once again. He was beginning to feel like a brush salesman, he thought, going through the same fruitless questionings. What had he accomplished so far? Not a thing. Not a single thing. He had used up a lot of gasoline and a lot of time and a lot of shoe leather, but Bob McKay was just as thoroughly under suspicion of murder as he had ever been, and no opening was presenting itself.

"Mrs. Lawrence, I believe?"

"That's right," she said suspiciously.

He smiled. "My name is Lowry, Ned Lowry. I'm from the *Gazette*."

The woman was looking at him in puzzled surprise.

"It's about Bob McKay," he went on.

She looked as though she understood why he was here now.

"Yes," she said. "Dr. Clayton's car was stolen right in front of the door here. The police have already been here."

"I know," he said. "Do you mind if I come in and talk with you for a while?"

"Yes, come in."

He followed her into a room crammed with furniture that looked too heavy for the narrow space and gave off the musty smell of overstuffed mohair. In a corner of the room a child lay uneasily asleep in a crib. The child was thin, pale, unlovely.

The woman asked him to sit down. Lowry lowered himself into a creaking overstuffed armchair. The woman sat down facing him. One of the middle buttons of her blouse was open, but she did not seem to notice. She seemed glad to sit down.

21

"That night, Mrs. Lawrence," Lowry began. "How did you happen to call Dr. Clayton?"

She looked sadly in the direction of the crib, a glance that told Lowry a great deal. The columnist felt sorry for her. There are tragedies outside of saloons and dance halls, he thought. Small tragedies, except for the people crushed by them. And people simply like to read about the saloon tragedies, not about the other kinds. That was why he wrote about them.

"He has asthma," she said. "A bad kind, the doctor says. He'll choke to death some night when I'm asleep, I know it."

There were tears in her eyes.

"I'm sorry to hear that," Lowry said.

"We haven't much money."

He admired the fortitude that showed in the understatement.

"I've been taking him to the clinic," she went on. "We couldn't afford to have a private doctor, of course. Dr. Clayton was the one who took care of him at the clinic most of the time."

"I see."

"When he got that terrible attack that night I didn't know what to do. I was afraid to pick him up and rush to the hospital. I had no money to pay a doctor with. I was desperate. I called Dr. Clayton and told him what happened. He was very sweet and said he would come. He saved my baby's life, I think."

"What time did he come?"

"About three in the morning, I guess. I don't know exactly. It seemed like the night had lasted for a million years."

"You were very anxious while you were waiting," Lowry said.

"I was dying with the baby," she said with sharp brevity.

Lowry kept his voice gentle, trying not to upset her. "You must have been looking through the window every once in a while to see if the doctor were coming, weren't you?"

"Yes. I was up and back a million times."

"Did you see anybody around the house, anybody on the street?"

"No, but McKay got into the car after the doctor parked it," she said. "He needn't have been around here before then."

"Not McKay," Lowry snapped irritably, nearly losing his temper at the woman's calm assumption of his friend's guilt.

"I beg your pardon," Mrs. Lawrence said. Despite the shabbiness of the house and her own worn condition, she drew herself up haughtily, insulted at his contradiction.

"I'm sorry," Lowry said. "You see, I don't think that man who did the killing and stole the car was McKay. It makes me angry to hear it."

"Oh," she said indifferently. McKay's tragedy didn't mean a thing to her. She had too many woes of her own to care very much about anybody else's.

"When the doctor arrived," Lowry said, "he took care of the baby and left. You didn't happen to see him to the door, did you?"

"No, I stayed close to the baby."

She was getting impatient. Lowry realized that in a few minutes she would probably ask him to leave. He had taken up plenty of her time already.

He rose wearily and looked in the direction of the crib.

In a gentle voice he asked, "How's he been feeling lately?"

She shrugged in a gesture of eloquent hopelessness. "They keep coming back, those attacks. They'll kill him yet. I know it, he'll never live to be old enough to walk or talk." The tears came to her eyes again.

"Bad attacks like the one he had that night—he's been having them since the doctor was here?"

"Only one more like the one he had that night, thank God."

Lowry sat down again. The woman looked at him peculiarly.

"When was that?" he asked with new urgency in his voice.

"One night about a week after the other one, I guess."

"And did you call Dr. Clayton again?"

"Yes, but I suppose I was expecting too much from him. He couldn't come out here that night. He said it would be all right if I carried the baby to the hospital. But I was afraid. It was a cold night and I didn't want the baby to catch a chill. I begged the doctor to come out here. He hung up on me. I can't blame him for that. We never could pay him anything. And it was awfully late, like the last time."

"What did you do?"

"I could only do one thing. I wrapped the baby up and took him down to the hospital. They took care of him. He was practically purple all over by the time I got there."

Lowry got up again and started toward the door. "Thanks awfully," he said. "You've been a great help to me, Mrs. Lawrence. I'm grateful for the time you've just spent. And I hope the baby feels better."

He contemplated giving her some money. But he decided against it. She was a poor woman, but she had her pride, and it would only humiliate and anger her if he handed her money. It was far better to mail her some cash in a plain envelope. Maybe she would know who it was from, but more likely she would just regard it as a gift from God.

As he moved to the door she asked curiously, "You think this man McKay is innocent?"

"Yes."

She shook her head. "Everybody has his own troubles, I guess."

Lowry found Brady at headquarters. The latter was in an uncommonly good mood when Lowry came upon him in the detectives' room.

"You must have been catching up on your sleep lately, Brady," Lowry said. "You look like a contented cat or something."

"Sit down, Lonelyhearts," Brady said. "Things are just sort of quiet around here for a change. Can't say that I mind it, either, this way. It kind of gives a guy a chance to breathe."

"You mean nobody's up there hollering 'get that man' because you just got one, eh?"

"Something like that."

"I figured that was what you were grinning about. You're pretty damn proud of yourself, I'll bet."

"You still don't think McKay's the man, do you, Lowry?"

"Less than ever."

Brady wasn't impressed by Lowry's statement. He leaned back and yawned extravagantly.

"Seriously, Brady," Lowry said. "Would you give McKay just the thousandth part of a break if it were possible?"

Brady's rugged jaw came forward like an advancing army tank.

"Take a tip from me, Lowry. It's finished. Forget all about it."

"I'm not asking for tips. Would you give him a break if it were possible? Or are you so anxious to send somebody to the gas chamber for the Blair murder that you don't give a hoot in hell whether the man you send is the right one or not?"

Brady's eyes grew cold. "I think he's the right man or I wouldn't have pulled him in."

"Sure, you *think* he is. But do you *know*? Do you want his death on your conscience forever?"

Brady scowled. "Listen, Lowry, don't come in here to heckle me. What is it you want?"

"Tell me, have you checked all of Doris Blair's boyfriends?"

"Yeah," Brady said. "Including McKay."

"Where did she go with those guys?"

Brady shrugged. "You try to dig that out, Lowry. What the devil do you think hotel registers tell, anyway?"

"Nothing."

"Exactly."

"Carrol wouldn't have had to go to hotels with her," Lowry said.

"Carrol wouldn't have had to go anyplace with her. McKay was doing the going during the period we're interested in."

"A nice sugar daddy McKay was. Rolling in wealth. Driving around in a new Cadillac every Monday. Just the sort to keep Doris the way she wanted to be kept, eh, Brady?"

"He didn't need money," Brady said. "It must have been love. They sat in cars and looked at the moon."

"But before you pulled McKay in you had been checking hotels and apartments."

Brady bit off the end of a cigar. He lit it slowly and took several deep puffs, allowing the columnist to wait impatiently.

He said finally, "Yeah. There was nothing in it. I tell you this must have been romance, Lowry. I don't even think the Blair girl had been seeing anybody for some time except this lug. We went over every hotel they generally go to. There wasn't a thing. Not a single solitary goddam thing, Lowry."

Lowry locked his hands together. "Seriously, Brady, if I find what you couldn't, would you at least take a look-see at it? Or do you have your heart set on railroading that poor son of a bitch?"

Brady blew another cloud of smoke arrogantly toward the ceiling.

"Okay, Lonelyhearts," he said without interest. "I'll do you that much of a favor. I'll listen to you if you come up with anything. But you can save yourself the exercise. You won't find a thing."

"Let me worry about that, Brady."

"It's all yours."

22

There was a fresh liveliness in Lowry's step as he went to his car again. He drove on a few blocks, pulling up outside of a drugstore. The phone booth was in the back. He waited impatiently until a bulky woman who was monopolizing the phone booth finally found herself able to tear herself away from the telephone. He lifted his hat as he brushed hastily past her and sat down in the booth.

He dialed Terry's number. She picked up before the phone had finished its first ring.

"Boy!" he exclaimed. "You must have been sitting right on top of the phone."

"Hello, Ned. I've been waiting to hear from you for so long."

"I'll pick you up in about twenty minutes," he told her. "How does this sound? We'll go for a ride in the country."

"What?" Terry asked in surprise.

"The fresh air will do you good, Terry," Lowry said. "Believe me."

"I don't get you. Just drop everything and go for a drive?"

"I know it seems heartless at a time like this," Lowry said. "But perhaps we can mix the pleasure with a little business. It won't be entirely a joyride. I've got something in mind."

"I figured you had. It isn't like you to take joyrides for their own sake."

"Well? Are you with me?"

"I guess so, Ned. I wasn't doing anything but biting my nails anyway just now. What sort of business do you mean?"

"I don't know yet."

"But—"

"Trust me, Terry. And don't ask questions. You'll understand soon enough."

"Okay."

"I'll be right over. So long."

Terry was ready to leave when he arrived at her apartment. The light-colored sports suit she wore seemed to blend with her pallor. She looked trim and neat. But so very pale.

Lowry frowned as he looked at her. "You need some fresh air, young lady," he said sternly. "If you weren't so beautiful I'd be tempted to say you need a doctor, Terry."

"Oh, really—"

"I mean it. Beautiful people never really look desperately sick. Nobody ever thinks of T.B. germs and sputum tests when he sees *Camille*."

"I'm all right," she said as she got into the automobile next to him.

He turned the key.

"I can see that," he replied drily.

The car began to move.

"Where are we going?" she asked.

"Patience, my child. Be patient and all will be revealed to you."

Driving with keen intensity, Lowry cut through as many side streets as he could, without going too much out of the way, and thus he managed to avoid a large part of the slow-moving city traffic.

Soon the road was a little less cluttered with cars and trucks and it was not very much longer before the oil wells around Long Beach came into view, thrusting up toward the blue sky in all their black, stark skeletonic ugliness. They reached the coast highway finally and to their right lay a smooth, unruffled sea.

Terry leaned back languidly in her seat and closed her eyes.

"Take some deep breaths," Lowry said. "A little fresh air in the lungs is the best medicine there is."

The car hummed along at fifty miles an hour. The warm sun and the fresh, salt smell began to relieve the tightness of Terry's nerves. This was good country out here. It hadn't been spoiled by the smog, the automobiles, the multitudes exploding out of Los Angeles.

"Where are we going?" she asked.

"Due south," Lowry answered vaguely. "Not awfully far."

"You're plenty mysterious."

"I know," he said. "I've chased so many bubbles, I don't want to give this a chance to become one. I want this to pan out the right way."

As he spoke he pressed down on the accelerator eagerly. They heard the raucous beeping of a horn behind them. Lowry throttled down, muttering something about California drivers, and let a flashy maroon sports car race past them. It streaked ahead for about fifty feet, then eased into the side of the road and remained in front.

"Did you see who was in that car that just rocketed past us?" Lowry asked.

"No," Terry said. "He went by a lot too fast for me to see anything."

"Take a guess."

"Winston Churchill?"

"Guess again."

"Marlene Dietrich?"

Lowry shook his head. "You're getting colder. I'll give you just one more try."

"Kaiser Wilhelm?" she asked.

"Wrong. It was your former boss."

Her eyes widened in surprise. "Carrol, you mean?"

"Who else?"

She laughed bitterly. "Don't tell me *he's* a lover of the wide open spaces, too."

Lowry shrugged. "I doubt it. Not after years of saloon life. He's accustomed to breathing an atmosphere of stale beer and cheap perfume."

"Do you think he saw us?" Terry asked anxiously, clenching her fists in unvoiced hatred of the man in the car ahead of her.

"I don't think so," Lowry said. "And I hope not. This is going to save me from asking a lot of questions about directions from the natives, unless I miss my guess about our friend up there."

Terry shook her head in complete mystification. "What's happening, Ned? I'm all confused. Why won't you tell me?"

"It won't be long now, Terry."

She glanced at him, but he had clammed up, and it was obvious he wasn't going to tell her one thing more until he was good and ready to. Terry crossed her legs, keeping her skirt from riding too high above her knee, and leaned back, breathing deeply. She remembered how the man in the car ahead of her had tried to rape her, and she shuddered with disgust, almost hoping that Carrol would have a blowout and die in a soaring leap from the road.

Lowry had to step up to sixty to keep Carrol's high-powered sports car in sight. As the miles ticked off on the odometer, the sea became a deeper blue. Rolling brown hills appeared in the east.

They slowed down to pass through a quiet village street, flanked by stumpy pineapple palms. When they were on the open road again, Carrol was driving even faster. Lowry brought his foot down sharply on the accelerator. The car spurted ahead.

"If the speed cops are drinking beer instead of watching the road, which they probably are, we'll get away with this," Lowry said.

"Won't you please tell me why you're following him?" Terry asked.

"I'm working on the theory that a saloon man like Carrol doesn't just like to drive in the country for the sake of fresh air."

"You mean you think he's going where you wanted to go?"

Lowry chuckled. "I guess a man just can't keep any secrets from you, Terry."

The road swerved inland and the ocean disappeared from sight for a long while. When they saw it again, the coast had turned rough, broken by sharply indented rocky coves. Thick clusters of straggly trees grew not ten yards from the narrow beaches, bent and twisted by the endless ocean winds.

Lowry stayed far enough behind Carrol's maroon sports car to avoid notice. They came to a neatly laid out town, tiny, touristy. Store windows on either side of the wide main street had pinkish, rough wood paneling. There were numerous art and curio shops. Artisans who made custom-built riding boots, saddles, boat models, picture frames, and all manner of other luxury craft goods displayed English signs over their doors. Everything about the town was very "arty and crafty."

The street was quiet except for a few elderly people standing about under the palms or else strolling but not seeming to be going anyplace in particular. From the main street Lowry and Terry were able to see the quiet waves breaking on the beach, which lay at the foot of the low cliff on which the little town appeared to have been built.

Carrol had slowed down to pass through the town. Another car got between them, but Lowry kept the maroon car in sight, and as soon as he could he passed the intervening car. As they came out of the town, Carrol once again began to pick up speed. They were driving along the oceanfront again.

About two miles down, Lowry saw Carrol take a turn to the right toward the beach. He nodded in satisfaction. "That's what I'd figure him to be doing," he said. "We're in luck, Terry."

"I wish I understood—"

"You will, honey. Just be patient."

Lowry began to crawl along at fifteen miles an hour. When they came to the point where Carrol had turned, they saw a short, sandy road leading to the beach. There was a low, white stucco house almost on the sand of the beach, surrounded by transplanted palms and shrubs. Carrol's car was parked at one side of the drive. Lowry pulled in behind it.

"You stay here, Terry," he said. "This isn't going to take very long."

"Like hell I will," she retorted. "You think I want to get sunstroke?"

"You may be safer out here."

"I'm coming in there with you, Ned."

Lowry shrugged. Terry followed him out of the car and they went up the short walk to the house. It was terribly quiet all around, except for the subdued sound of the beating of the surf on the shore.

Carrol had left the front door open. They walked in, finding themselves in a cool, low-ceilinged room, furnished in soft, cream-colored fabrics. There were bookshelves lined with novels along one wall, and a small spinet-type piano.

"Listen," Terry whispered.

She pointed toward the interior of the house. The sound of footsteps moving around on a wooden floor could plainly be heard. Lowry put his hand on Terry's shoulder. He stared levelly at her. "You're the one who wanted to come in with me. Do you feel like a tough guy, Terry?"

She nodded her head quickly.

Lowry's smile was tense and brief. "Okay. I want you to go in there."

"With Carrol?"

He nodded. "When he starts blustering, say anything that comes into your head, just to stall him until I can get in behind him. Okay?"

"Okay."

"He'll probably have whatever he came for by now. Go on. I'll be waiting."

He slapped her shoulder gently. She smiled back, trying to display a courage she did not feel, and tiptoed out into the hall that led to the other rooms. Lowry followed her and stood in the doorway, listening.

23

Terry walked quietly forward, through the attractively furnished house. Her heart pounded. What if he had a gun? What if he seized her and somehow killed Lowry? She pictured herself alone in this house with Carrol, way out here at the edge of nowhere, as the big ugly man ripped off her clothes and savagely wrought his will on her naked body, grasping with his filthy hands at her flesh—

There he was. The door to the bedroom was open, and, looking in, she could see him. It was a large room like the other with a wide maple bed and a floor that was bare except for an Indian scatter rug. Terry saw Carrol lying on the floor, half under the bed, only his legs sticking out. She hadn't made any noise coming in and Carrol apparently hadn't heard anything.

She waited.

After a moment Carrol began to wriggle out from under the bed. He stood up, holding a tiny green object in his hand. Then, realizing he was not alone, he wheeled suddenly and faced her. The astonishment in his face quickly gave place to the nasty scowl she had seen once before.

"What—you—" he grunted.

"Looking for an old maid under the bed?" she asked flippantly.

"You little bitch, you've been following me around," he said thickly. Carrol's hand went to his pocket and came out with a short-barreled revolver.

"Your nose is in it this time for fair, sister," he said. "Get away from that door."

He gestured with the gun. Trembling a little, Terry moved slowly into the room. Carrol kept the gun leveled at her and walked watchfully to the place where she had stood. His eyes were hard and bitter, and seemed to be undressing her. Once again, brutish animal lust was radiating from him.

"I'm gonna leave you here, sister," he said. "And nobody'll ever know the difference. I'll have the fun I didn't get the other time, and then I'll make sure you can't cry to the cops about it. It's all right with me if you like McKay enough to risk your neck, but you're steppin' out of bounds tanglin' with me."

Terry's throat was dry with terror. But her eyes were on the green object in Carrol's hand. She forced herself to be calm, telling herself that she had to stall until Lowry could help her.

"That's a lovely earring," she said with a mirthless smile. "But they sell for about a dollar a pair and that's only one of them. Doesn't seem worth making a fifty-mile trip for, really."

"I could tell you all about this earring," Carrol said coldly. "But it won't do you any good to know. You know too much already." He tossed the green earring lightly into the air and caught it. Then his gaze came to rest on the twin jutting mounds of her bosom, and a hungry look sparkled in his eyes.

"Maybe I better not waste time with you," he mused aloud. "I can get plenty of it anywhere I want. But I better not stick around here too long." He shrugged. "A lousy shame. But it ain't worth risking. It would be fun to tumble you around, too." He shook his head. "I hate to do this, sister," he said coldly. "But I got a future to think about."

The hand with the gun came into a higher, more deadly position. Terry tried hard to shake off a sharp, sinking sensation. Then she saw Lowry in the doorway behind Carrol. There was a heavy bronze bookend in his hand. She looked quickly back at the gun but Carrol had caught the glance she had thrown behind him and he started to turn. Lowry brought the bookend down on Carrol's head and Carrol hit the floor with a thud. The gun fell to the carpet and Lowry kicked it aside.

"Lincoln," Lowry said, holding the bookend up to display the carved head of the Great Emancipator on one side.

The sinking sensation became too much for Terry to cope with. She sat limply down on the bed.

There was a trickle of blood at the back of Carrol's head. Lowry bent over him.

"I didn't hit him awfully hard," he said apologetically. He took the green earring from Carrol's hand and came over to sit beside Terry.

"Are you all right?" he asked anxiously. "You worked beautifully."

"I'm all right," she said weakly.

"I'll see if I can dig up a drink," he said. "But first I think I'll tie our pal up. He's troublesome when he's loose."

He went out and came back with a roll of line cord.

"Found it in the garage," he said.

He bent over Carrol again.

"I used to be a boy scout once. Hope I remember the knots."

He tied Carrol's hands behind him, then wound some rope around his feet and made half a dozen knots.

"We really ought to hang him," he said. "He didn't mind knowing Bob would get what's poetically known as the supreme penalty and he knew all the time it wasn't Bob. He'll keep here for the time being. Now let's get that drink if there's one around. You not only need it, you deserve it."

He led Terry into the living room. There was a cabinet which he opened.

"Rye," he said. "Like rye?"

"If it has alcohol in it, it'll do," she said. "I came near fainting, I suppose."

"Terry," he said reproachfully. "Not you."

He went out to the kitchen and returned with two glasses.

"Drink it down fast," he said. "It'll work wonders."

She swallowed the drink and sat down in one of the big, summery chairs.

"Better?" Lowry asked.

"Much better," she said. "Then that was it. I was right."

Lowry looked at the earring in his hand.

"Think it's pretty?" he asked.

"A little on the flashy side," she said. "But it depends on who wears it."

"Doris would have looked all right with it on, I guess."

"Why was he suddenly so worried about a missing earring?"

"I'll be able to tell you in about an hour, Terry. Where do you suppose the phone is?"

"Right behind you."

Lowry turned around. There was a telephone on the table.

"My powers of observation are marvelous," he said.

Lowry gave the operator a number. Terry looked around the room admiringly.

"Imagine a mug like Carrol having a lovely place like this. He must have paid an interior decorator a small fortune or do you think there's a side to him nobody knows about?"

"No," Lowry said. "And I can't imagine him having a place like this." He turned to the phone. "I want Detective Sergeant Brady," he said into the mouthpiece.

Terry listened as Lowry spoke.

"Hello, Brady," he was saying. "Remember what you said. Get Dr. Clayton. Tell him I've caught Carrol burglarizing his beach home. Bring him down here. He may want to see what's missing. No, Brady, I'm not being a wise guy. You said you'd give us a break. Well, this is it. Be a sport, will you, old man? That's a good fellow. I'll expect you in about an hour."

Lowry put the phone back in its cradle. "We can have another drink now," he said. He poured more whiskey and sat down opposite Terry. "Read any good books lately?" he asked.

"Ned," she said. "Then this isn't Carrol's place."

"No."

"Then what was he doing?"

"Looking for an earring, apparently."

"But why?"

"We'll have to wait until he wakes up to ask him. By the way, I think I'll see how he's getting along."

He finished his drink, set the empty glass down, and went into the bedroom.

Carrol lay just as he had left him. His face was white but the blood had stopped running at the back of his head. Lowry bent over him and listened to his faint breathing.

Terry came in.

"Is he all right?" she asked.

Lowry nodded. "Yes, he's all right. Just a bit the worse for wear. If I'd slugged him a little harder I guess I would have saved him a lot of the trouble he's going to run into now. I'll see if I can manage to fix him up a little." He went into the bathroom and returned a moment later with a wet towel. Kneeling, he began to bathe Carrol's head.

"Get him a drink, won't you, Terry?" he said. "It'll perk him up."

Terry poured a glass of the rye and brought it in. Lowry put it to Carrol's lips. In a little while Carrol began to stir. A low moan came from his wide mouth. Then he lay still again.

"He's out again," Terry said.

"He'll come out of it after a while," Lowry remarked. "Though probably Brady will have him this way again in a very short time."

Lowry took a pillow from the bed and put it on the floor under Carrol's head.

Standing up, he said, "That's more than he'd have done for us. But they call me big-hearted Lowry, you know."

"No, I didn't."

"Well, now you do. We can leave him alone. He'll get along all right."

They sat down in the living room again.

"Do you think he'd have shot me?" Terry asked.

"I wouldn't put it past him."

"I guess I was lucky."

"Luckier than some," Lowry said.

Within an hour, they heard the wail of a siren outside.

"There they are," Lowry said. He remained seated without making a move to get up.

Brady, followed by Harrison and Dr. Clayton, came in through the open door. Two uniformed policemen followed them. Brady looked suspiciously from Lowry to Terry. "Well, what's it about?" he snapped.

Lowry looked up at Dr. Clayton and said, "I hope you don't mind the fact that we made ourselves comfortable in your place, Doctor. Your rye is excellent. We were sure you'd understand."

"Of course," Clayton said magnanimously. He favored Lowry with a warm, friendly smile. "I don't understand about this robbery," he said. "Just how did you happen on it?"

Lowry studied the doctor's handsome, dignified features.

"We were taking a drive," he said. "We came down this way to have a look at the ocean in this lovely weather. And we saw this man breaking into the house. I'm a very nosy person, you know, Dr. Clayton. It's something of a professional trait, you might say. And so I just had to see what was happening."

"You're telling us," Brady growled unpleasantly. "Where is he?"

"Inside."

24

Lowry and Terry followed the others to the bedroom. Carrol was still sprawled out, seemingly sleeping in utter tranquility. "You slugged him," Brady said immediately to Lowry, in tones of reproach.

"Very unfortunate circumstances required me to," Lowry said solemnly. "It was absolutely necessary, or I never would have done it. Cross my heart and hope to die, Brady, old man."

Dr. Clayton got down on one knee and scrutinized the slumbering Carrol.

"He'll be all right," he said after a brief examination. "I think I can fix him up."

"All right, go to it, Doctor," Brady said. Turning to Harrison, he said, "Suppose we have a look around here while the doc's working."

Brady, Harrison, and the uniformed men went back to the living room. Lowry and Terry looked on as Dr. Clayton ministered with efficient skill to Carrol. After a few moments the stunned man opened his eyes and looked dazedly about him.

"Lowry," Brady called loudly from the other room. "Come on in here, will you? I want to talk to you. And bring the girlfriend, too." Lowry and Terry went to the living room. "Did you tail Carrol here?" Brady asked, his eyes unfriendly.

"More or less," Lowry said. "We were on our way here ourselves when we spotted Carrol. We just followed him and he led us right to the door."

"And why were you coming here? A little more of your amateur sleuthing?"

"Well—" Lowry started to say.

But the sentence was cut abruptly short after the first word. A shot rang out from the bedroom like the sharp, throaty bark of a big dog.

"Carrol!" Brady yelled.

The policemen dashed pell-mell to the bedroom. Lowry followed at a somewhat more leisurely pace. Terry grasped his arm and went along with him.

It was not a pretty sight.

Dr. Clayton was bending over the fallen Carrol. The top of Carrol's head was a hideous mess of scrambled blood and bone. His hand lay outstretched at his side, and in it was clasped the gun which he had earlier pointed at Terry. The line cord, wrenched apart, still hung from his wrists.

"I started to go to the bathroom to wet this towel," Dr. Clayton said, rising and holding out the towel. "But just as I got there and reached for the faucet, I heard the shot." Brady covered the revolver with a handkerchief and took it from Carrol's lifeless hand. He slipped it into his pocket.

Lowry came close to Clayton.

"It's too bad you didn't wear gloves, Dr. Clayton. Because the only fingerprints they're going to find on that gun will be Carrol's and yours. I should have remembered to take that gun away, but I guess I thought Carrol was in no condition to use it anyway. And he's a small loss in any case."

"Yes, naturally," Clayton said, maintaining his assured, dignified professional manner. "My fingerprints will be on the gun, certainly. I touched it hoping to take it away before he might have a chance to shoot again. I didn't realize at first that he'd succeeded in killing himself immediately."

Lowry's laugh was short and contemptuous. "Oh, come off it, doc. You don't even have to be a freshman in medical school to realize a man is dead when his head looks like that," Lowry said deliberately.

Brady had edged close to Clayton, too, by this time. The expression on his face was a cold one.

"This time Lowry's right, for a change, Dr. Clayton," Brady said. "Carrol was out here at your place for something you didn't think he ought to know about, wasn't he?"

"I'm sure I don't have the faintest notion of what you're talking about," Clayton said stiffly, glowering at both men.

"I'll try to make it as plain as possible," Lowry said with heavy sarcasm. He took the green earring from his pocket and held it up, moving it back and forth in front of Clayton's eyes.

"Remember this particular little bauble, Dr. Clayton?" he asked.

Clayton's face was an impassive mask. "Of course not," he said.

"Of course you do, you mean. Permit me to refresh your memory a little. A man of your professional stature has so much on his mind that occasionally he lets a little detail slip out of his memory. But I'll fill in the blank for you, doctor. Your little companion, Doris Blair, used to wear this earring. It matched a light green evening gown of hers. Remember?"

"Hey, lemme see that!" Brady yelled. He took the earring from Lowry's hand and inspected it closely. Looking up, he said, "We've got the mate to this. Found it with all the rest of her junk. We wondered about the singleton for a while."

"But not long enough," Lowry said icily. "It was less work just to pinch McKay."

"Can that," Brady said angrily. "You didn't know so much yourself. You were just bluffing right along the whole time."

"Now, see here," Dr. Clayton said, his expression becoming one of irritation. "I don't know what you fellows think you're about, but if this is some kind of an attempt at humor I might as well tell you that I don't think it's awfully funny."

"Let me assure you, doctor," Lowry said, "that this is definitely not an attempt at humor. Dr. Clayton, it didn't do you a single bit of good to shoot Carrol. Your number was up long before that, whether you realized it or not."

He turned to Brady. "Carrol found that earring right here under the bed. We caught him just as he finished squirreling around down there to find it. It seems Dr. Clayton thought he was in the clear with McKay's trial coming up so soon and everything looking so damning against him. So he figured that the blackmail he was paying Carrol to shut up was really a waste of money. That was what was on your mind, wasn't it, Dr. Clayton? Don't try to bluff."

Clayton's lips were drawn together in a tight, grim line. His face had turned deathly pale. He did not speak.

Lowry nodded. "You'd better hold still, doctor. That's a lot more sensible than all the business of righteous indignation that you were pulling a little while ago."

Lowry turned to Brady. "You see, Brady, up to this time all that Carrol had to go on was one bit of information: the knowledge that Dr. Clayton was the boyfriend who was supposed to be giving Doris Blair the life of luxury she craved in return for the favors of her lily-white body. That was enough to make Dr. Clayton pay up, but, as I said, it began sooner or later to seem to him that with McKay taking the rap he had nothing to worry about anymore. So he must have told Carrol where to head on the blackmail deal. You still with me, Brady?"

"Go ahead," the detective said tightly.

"Imagine Carrol's position. It was his word against Dr. Clayton's if he decided to go to the police with the story. The word of a shady character like Carrol against that of a highly respected member of the community like the doctor. Besides, Carrol wasn't interested in going to the police. That wouldn't have netted much for *him*. What he was really interested in was getting a way to squeeze more blackmail money out of the doctor. So he came here in the hope that he'd find some concrete evidence with which he could frighten Dr. Clayton into paying more money. I forgot about the gun and you gentlemen didn't notice it. It was an awful mistake to have left Dr. Clayton alone with Carrol for those few minutes. Dr. Clayton thought Carrol was the only man who stood between him and his freedom."

Brady and the police were watching Dr. Clayton. They were all watching him as he began to crumble, as the firm, strong mouth began to twitch nervously, as the handsome features began to lose their rigidity and grow slack with fear. His shoulders drooped a little now. He only resembled the man who had come into the house a little earlier.

"You're beginning to look a little tired, Dr. Clayton," Lowry said. "I don't wonder. The going is getting tough, isn't it? I can't feel sorry for you. To be blunt you're a cold-blooded sort of louse. You strangled Doris Blair because she was demanding that you treat her as you promised instead of keeping her in a back alley. You wanted Doris Blair but you also wanted to be sure that there would be no interference with your smug respectability. Doris must have threatened to air your romance and you didn't like that. Next you did a dandy job of identifying an innocent man, made it look as if you weren't quite certain about him which always makes an identification seem more honest. And just now when it looked like Carrol would finally wreck everything anyway, you only took a few seconds to decide to blow the top of his head off."

Brady put his hand on Clayton's arm. As Lowry looked on,

he saw Brady's heavy, pugnacious jaw come forward in the manner that meant he was going to become businesslike in the only business he knew well.

Brady gave Clayton a violent shake. The doctor wobbled as if all his joints had suddenly been separated and strung on with wire.

"He's right, ain't he, Clayton," Brady growled savagely. "That was the way it was. Or do you have some better answer?"

Clayton made no reply. The look of hunted futility in his eyes said plainly that he realized it was useless to talk.

Brady shook him again, more violently this time. "Come on. Speak up."

"Yes," Clayton said in a low voice, nodding his head slowly. He looked dreadfully pale. The starch had gone out of him completely.

Brady turned to one of the uniformed men. "You stay here and watch this bird," he said. "I'll phone the locals and let them know they can take over for us."

Brady went to the phone and quickly put in the call to the local police. Hanging up, he nodded in satisfaction and said, "We can go now."

Harrison and the other cop took Dr. Clayton with them in the police car.

"You mind if I ride back with you?" Brady asked Lowry, a trifle sheepishly.

"A pleasure, Sergeant Brady," Lowry said with hearty magnanimity.

Terry sat snugly between Lowry and Brady in the front seat of Lowry's car. She darted a cold, unfriendly look at Brady, who winced.

"You must hate me," he said.

"She isn't head over heels in love with you, Brady, if that's what you mean. But you've got to forgive him, Terry. He was only doing his job."

"That's right, Ma'am."

"His job says that for every murder there has to be an apprehended murderer," Lowry says. "Too many unsolved crimes and something mysterious happens to Sergeant Brady's next promotion. It's a nasty setup, Terry. But it's a nasty world we live in."

Terry said nothing. She could not yet bring herself to forgive the man who had so energetically tried to send Bob to the gas chamber, but on the other hand she could not fully hate him either.

As they drove through the little town with the cozy art shops, Lowry said, "Isn't Laguna a lovely town, so quaint, so artistic and stuff?"

"Yeah," Brady said. "How'd you get the idea about Laguna?"

"And the rest of the ideas," Lowry teased. "That was why you wanted to ride back with us, Brady. You wanted to find out what it is that makes smart detectives tick."

"All right," Brady grunted. "Be a wise guy. See if I care. How'd you piece all this together?"

They were coming through the other side of the town now. The sun was beginning to sink on the horizon. The sea had changed from its deep blue color to a dark shade of green.

"Nothing to it, Brady," Lowry said. "If you don't get scared that the public is going to start beefing about what's the matter with our police force and pull in the first sucker who looks like he might have been guilty and won't have much fight in him. But I won't rub that in now. First, I suppose it was important that I never believed it was McKay because I knew he couldn't have had any part in Doris Blair's life. Both Ramirez' identification of him and Clayton's were made under such unbelievable circumstances that I knew there could be nothing to them. The first inkling we had of the name of the man who had been mixed up with Doris was when one of Carrol's girls told Terry that Doris used to speak of a man whom she called Buzzy. Doris' landlady had heard of Buzzy, too. You probably had heard about Buzzy but you assumed Buzzy must have been McKay, didn't you?"

"Yeah," Brady said sourly.

"Well, women will think up some strange nicknames for men but Buzzy was Dr. Clayton. For a little while it looked like Carrol might have been Buzzy, especially as it seemed from the experience of our little friend here that Carrol selected the most attractive of his current crop of girls to be his own personal favorite, sort of like a sultan in his harem, you know. But there was something Doris' landlady told us that seemed to eliminate Carrol. That was the last time Buzzy had called Doris had been on a Friday and then she hadn't turned up all weekend. That meant a tryst some place together and weekends are when Carrol takes in most of his money at the bar and when he's needed there the most. It didn't seem as if he'd leave his flourishing business even for love.

"You probably don't know about Miss Stafford's experience with Carrol but it happened that he became very worried about the investigating she was doing and favored her with a call which also ended disastrously for him. That too made it look as if Carrol might have been the man as he was obviously afraid that Terry knew something. The answer to that is now that since he was blackmailing Clayton he couldn't afford to have any sort of leak which might lead to the doctor, first because that would end a valuable source of revenue to him and second because he must have known that in dealing with Clayton he was dealing with no softy and that if Clayton suspected he had told anything he wouldn't hesitate to get him.

"All these things still didn't point to Clayton, of course. If I had approached this properly to start with I could have reached Clayton sooner but I was worried primarily about McKay and how to get him out of the mess instead of how to solve the murder. That was unfortunate because a really smart detective could have found what was phony about Clayton very quickly, I think."

"When?" Brady interrupted.

"Almost as soon as the investigating began."

"How do you figure that out?"

"This way. Clayton's story was that when he came out of a patient's house there was somebody waiting in the back of his car who held him up. This man, according to him, took his wallet and stole his car which he intended to use to drive off with a girl and murder her. Having committed the crime of robbery and planning the crime of murder, he was still indifferent enough to expose his face completely to the one man who might later identify him if anything went wrong when it would have been the simplest thing in the world to cover his face with a handkerchief, Jesse James style."

"Something in that," Brady conceded.

"And most important of all was the way you neglected the element of the patient Clayton was seeing at three o'clock in the morning. Didn't it ever occur to you that it was odd that a fashionable doctor from Westwood Hills should make a call at three o'clock in the morning on a charity patient in a slum? Do they generally do that sort of thing? Not many of them, I'd say."

"You mean he didn't call on a patient? The Lawrence woman said he did. What would her angle be?"

"He did call on a patient. He most certainly did. It was the finest pretext in the world to be in the neighborhood of Carrol's Bar at the hour when the girls were leaving. It probably also furnished a swell story for his wife. When he finished with the patient he was just in time to meet Doris Blair and take her for that ride. In answering that call he had a stall for his wife, for you fellows, for all of us. It came in nice and handy for him, you see, and I bet he felt smug about doing a good deed that helped him out plenty at the same time. But when Mrs. Lawrence's baby got sick again a week later, and she phoned him in the middle of the night to come out again, he refused to come. In fact, he even hung up on her. That was a big mistake. It proved that he wasn't all charity."

"You found that out?"

"Yes. Didn't you?" Lowry asked.

Brady looked shamefaced. "I got to admit we didn't pick up that point. We weren't interested in what happened a week later."

They drove along in silence for a while, each lost in his own thoughts.

Brady broke it finally. He asked, "How'd you manage to find out about the house in Laguna?"

Lowry smiled. "I knew if he were having an affair with Doris they must have been going someplace together. They weren't doing it in the treetops. You said you had checked all hotels and apartments and hadn't come up with anything worthwhile. And then his daughter tipped me off about the house in Laguna."

"His daughter?"

Lowry nodded. "Yes, a cute little girl, pretty as a picture. I feel pretty rotten about using her words as a hook to send her old man to the death chamber, but that's the way it goes."

"Where'd you find her?"

"I went to see Clayton this morning," Lowry explained. "I

was just going along on a hunch, trying to see if he could be made to realize that his testimony would send McKay to the lethal chamber. I didn't even begin to suspect him of being the man, then. I just wanted him to reconsider his testimony. I, too, was impressed with that doubt which Clayton seemed to have about McKay. I thought perhaps he really was being sincere about not being sure it was McKay he saw. Maybe, I figured, I could get him to back down and not seem so positive on the witness stand. I didn't know yet that his hesitation was part of his plan to make it seem authentic. On the other hand, there's always the likelihood to be considered that he did feel a little sorry to be sending an innocent man to the gas chamber for his crime. Perhaps he thought McKay might get off and he still wouldn't be involved. I don't know what he was thinking. But anyway, I went to talk to him, and after I left I met his child and his wife in the garden, and just for no reason at all I smiled and said hello. Cutest little child you want to see. Anyway, I was talking to the child. She said something about there being a summer house at Laguna. If the suspicions that began to pop into my mind were at all correct, then that would neatly take care of the problem of where Doris and her lover had been going. As it happens, I was right. The earring that Carrol found was probably lost there the last time they were there together. That was the time Doris' landlady was telling you about."

Brady was silent, lost in deep thought. The traffic was growing rapidly heavier now, and the police car in front of them was using the siren and speeding past the other cars. Lowry followed it closely.

In a little while they were back in town. They pulled up in front of headquarters.

Lowry looked at Terry. The hectic hours had taken their toll.

"You look tired again, Terry," he said. "I'll take you home now."

She shook her head. "I'm not as tired as all that. Could I possibly see Bob now, do you think?"

"Pretty soon," Brady said. There was the beginning of a faint smile on his granite physiognomy. "Take her home," he said to Lowry. "I'll call you in a little while. We're going to be wanting you some more before this is done, you know."

"I know," Lowry said cheerfully. He glanced at Terry. "You'd better go home and get some rest. Okay?"

25

In her apartment, half an hour later, Terry stretched out luxuriously on the divan while Lowry sat in a chair enjoying a stiff highball.

Terry smiled warmly. "I feel as if I'm just about to be born," Terry said. "Does that sound silly? Does it make any sense at all?"

"Sounds very real," Lowry said seriously.

The phone rang.

Terry leaped up, but Lowry waved her back. "I'll get it," he told her.

It was Brady. "That you, Lowry?"

"None other."

"I got to hand it to you, Lowry," Brady said. "You figured it right without one miss. We didn't even have to sweat him."

"Well, now, that's a crying shame, isn't it," Lowry said with heavy sarcasm. "I'll bet you boys were all broken up about that. You lost out on the chance to get your weekly quota of exercise."

Brady muttered something darkly unintelligible. Lowry didn't ask him to repeat it.

"What about McKay?" Lowry asked. "There's a girl here who's kind of interested in what's going to happen to him."

"There's an order out for his release. There'll be a little bit of red tape and then he'll walk out of here a free man."

"Glad to hear that," Lowry said.

Brady was awkwardly silent for a long moment. Lowry held the phone, making a sign with his thumb and forefinger to tell Terry that everything was all right.

After the pause, Brady said hesitantly, "Say, listen, Lowry—"

"Mmm?"

"Do you think McKay will sue for false arrest?"

"I really don't know," Lowry said delightedly. "It's hard to tell what kind of attitude a man will take when he's been put in a position like that."

"Well—er—you think you could get him to soft pedal a little? I mean, go easy on us? I'd be in a hell of a tough jam if he tried really to crack down on us, you know. But if you talked to him—"

"If I did," Lowry said thoughtfully, "what would there be in it for me?"

Brady paused again. "Well," he said finally, "we could do you some pretty big favors. Like giving you the run of the juiciest stories for 'The Seamy Side.' How's that?"

"Sounds good," Lowry said casually. "Maybe I can get McKay to take it easy on you. Provided he isn't too sore at you, that is."

"Yeah," Brady said in a discouraged tone.

"Anything else?"

"No, that's it."

"See you around, Brady. Thanks for nothing."

Lowry hung up.

"Well?" Terry asked.

"Perfect," Lowry said. "They're letting him go as soon as possible. The doctor is the man."

"Wonderful!" Terry cried. She was up out of the chair at a bound. "Oh, how can I ever thank you, Ned? It's been so grand of you to do all this for Bob—"

Suddenly, impulsively, she threw herself against him. Lowry opened his arms wide, more in surprise than anything else, and he felt the girl's warm presence against him, her lips seeking his.

They kissed quickly. And then it was over. She was stepping

back, and he was tingling from the contact. But that was all that there would ever be, he thought ruefully. She belonged to somebody else. He would just have to put the kiss into the old memory book, and let it go at that.

The dancers and those who just came to listen were in an ecstasy at the Lafayette. On the platform at the end of the dance floor, Bob McKay stood at the head of his orchestra, giving forth wild, bacchanalian music from his red-hot clarinet.

His face was flushed but joyous, and an unruly lock of blond hair shook back and forth across his forehead as his body from the waist up wove to and fro, back and forth in wild gyrations.

At a table near the dance floor, Lowry, Terry, and Max Dreiblatt, the owner of the Lafayette, sat listening attentively, each unconsciously beating time with his heels.

As the number reached the fever pitch that was the forerunner of the abrupt ending that would follow, Dreiblatt shook his head in wonder.

Lowry grinned at him. "You like it real big, huh, Max?" he asked.

"Can those boys ever give out, boy, oh boy!" Dreiblatt said rhapsodically. "That boy McKay is the best in the business. Bar none. Bar absolutely none."

"Looks like you've got a big turnout tonight to hear him, too."

Dreiblatt nodded happily. "Yep. The house is packed, Ned. It just goes to show you what a little bit of publicity will do."

"It works wonders, Max."

"It sure does," Dreiblatt agreed. "A guy goes to the can charged with murder. Then he gets out. So that packs them in to listen to him swing it. It makes them feel like they're celebrities themselves to come here."

"Also they know he's good."

Dreiblatt nodded. "He was always good, Ned. But a little publicity don't hurt."

The cornetist broke off the number on a half dozen nerve-shattering hot licks. McKay left the bandstand as the crowd cheered, and strode jauntily across the floor to the table.

Terry took his hand, gripping it tightly as though to make sure he would never ever go away from her.

"You were marvelous, Bob," she said.

McKay smiled broadly. "Thanks, honey. Whew! I'm a little warm."

As if on cue, a waiter came up with a tall glass, and placed it before McKay. Nodding gratefully, McKay picked the glass up and began sipping slowly.

"There's something about lemonade," he said. "So cool, refreshing. Like a pure mountain stream."

Lowry laughed. "And chock full of vitamins."

"I'm getting plenty of those these days," he said. "Ask Terry."

Dreiblatt rose. "Well, I got to see how things is goin'," he said.

When he had gone, Lowry rose, too.

"I'll be seeing you kids," he said.

"Come up to the house in the morning and have breakfast with us," Terry said.

"Don't kid me, lady. Besides I have other things to do besides playing dear Uncle Ned to a pair of newlywed lovebirds."

"Oh, a tough guy, huh?"

"I have to be," Lowry said gaily. "I'm going out among 'em now. Nothing ever happens here."

JAILBAIT GIRL

Originally published in the September, 1959 issue of
GUILTY DETECTIVE STORY MAGAZINE

It was a real sweet set-up, Janey thought. It was one of the niftiest, coolest cons anybody had ever thought up. She stood in front of the mirror, combing her hair, admiring the youthful beauty of her body.

Behind her Charley said, "Hurry it up. It's after eight. We want to catch our mark before it gets too late."

"Don't rush me," Janey said evenly. "I hate being rushed, Charley."

Deliberately and slowly she finished doing her hair, and reached for the filmy underthings lying crumpled on the bed. She smiled in pleasure at the sight of her nakedness in the mirror. Her body was lean but full in the places that counted, with firm, high breasts and flaring hips.

It was the body of a girl in the first ripeness of youth. When she wore her sweater-and-bobby-sox outfit and kept her hair in an adolescent-style ponytail, she could pass for being only sixteen or seventeen.

She knew how to turn on that dewy-eyed, virginal look. It was her biggest asset in trade. Actually she was almost twenty-three, but she could pass for sixteen any time she wanted to.

"Come *on*," Charley said impatiently, as she fumbled with her buttons.

She glared at him. "I tell you, I don't like to be rushed. Don't bug me, Charley, or I'll get sore at you. Remember, I can do this act without you, but you're nowhere without me."

"Is that a hint?"

"It ain't nothing. I'm just telling you not to get on my nerves. I gotta look cool for this performance tonight, you dope."

He sighed loudly but said nothing else until she was finished dressing. Right now she looked nothing like a teenager, with her hair done up fancy, her eyes darkened by makeup, her dress cut low in front to show her assets. This was going to be the fifth time in the last two months they had worked the gambit. So far they were four for four, a perfect batting average. It was easy to make the suckers come across, Janey thought. Most of them were down here alone to get away from their wives for a while, and the last thing in the world they wanted was to get hauled up on a statutory rape charge.

Of course, if somebody ever called their bluff—

Janey didn't like to think about that. But so far the gimmick had worked four out of four times. They had collected two thousand bucks. Another three or four operations, Janey thought, and they would have enough green stuff to pick up stakes and head out for California and the good life out there.

"Okay," she said to the patiently fuming Charley. "I'm ready now."

"Damn near about time."

"Remember what I said about getting me riled up?"

"Okay, okay. I'll lay off. You're pretty damn touchy tonight, though."

"I always am, just before an engagement."

They went downstairs, and out of the house. It was a cheap boarding house, and they paid fifteen bucks a week for their dingy two-room place. When they moved to California, Janey thought, they would get someplace nice to live in, and a nice car, and a lot of other nice things. Right now the two thousand bucks they had collected on their little sucker game was sitting in the bank, and they weren't touching it. That was their nest egg.

They got into the old rattletrap Ford that Charley had bought last year for eighty-five dollars and drove downtown to the big hotel district. That was the way they worked it. Janey dressed up and went wandering around the hotels, looking for a likely mark. She picked him up, went to his room, gave him a good time. Later that night Charley would show up and do the outraged brother act, and the mark would cough up five hundred smackers rather than get hooked into a statutory rape charge.

Four out of four, without a hitch. Janey remembered all four clearly. The first had been a bald-headed, potbellied stockbroker from New York. Then a playboy type from out west, with a red Jaguar and a little clipped mustache. After him, an accountant from Chicago, and then, last week, a middle-aged Milwaukee businessman. They had all coughed up the cash without too much of a squawk. They were all afraid of getting dragged into court.

Charley parked the car about a block from the elegant Boardwalk Plaza Hotel. The rickety little Ford looked pretty pathetic next to the massive Cadillacs and Imperials and foreign sports cars all over the place, but Janey told herself that someday they were going to have a fancy little car like that.

"Let's synchronize watches, Captain," Janey said with an impish smile.

"Right. It's quarter after eight now. Figure you'll pick up your mark by nine, at latest, and spend an hour in his room. You ought to be back here by ten; I'll be waiting for you."

"Okay," she said, and went teetering along toward the hotel on her high heels. Dressed as she was, in the expensive outfit that had been a necessary investment for this project, she looked like a high-quality B-girl. Without the makeup and the smart clothes, she could pass for a high school junior. It was a handy attribute to have, the ability to seem two different ages.

She walked into the hotel lobby. It was a swanky place, all plate glass and thick carpets. A glowing green sign said COCKTAIL LOUNGE, and she steered her course thataway, ignoring the genial leers of the bellhops standing around in the lobby.

The lounge was crowded—mostly with couples, as usual, but here and there Janey saw a single man drinking alone. She stood at the entrance for a moment, looking over the crop. It was very important for her to guess right the first time. This was a fashionable place, and the bartenders didn't want B-girls buzzing around from patron to patron. She would have to pick a winner the first time, or else clear out and try some other hotel along the tourist strip.

It didn't take her long to pick out her man. He was sitting at the far end of the bar, nursing what looked like a martini. He seemed to be young—in his late twenties or early thirties—but his forehead was very high, and most likely he was sensitive about losing his hair.

The best kinds were the sensitive ones, Janey had learned. This fellow wore sport clothes; he was tanned and broad-shouldered and pretty muscular, and he looked reasonably handsome except for the unfortunate thinning of his hair. More important, he also looked well-heeled.

Janey walked over to him.

There was a seat empty to his right. Janey smiled sweetly and said to him, "Mind if I sit down here?"

"Go right ahead," he said. His voice was deep and musical-sounding.

Janey wriggled into the seat, making sure to give him a good look at her bosom as she did so. The bra she was wearing molded her figure seductively, thrusting her breasts upward and out and putting them on display. And she had a classy figure, no doubt about it.

The bartender was busy about a dozen stools over. Janey

smiled at the man next to her and said, "Do they make a good martini here? Some of these hotels give you a so-called martini made up of one third gin, one third vermouth, and one third ice water, all for only ninety cents."

"This one isn't bad," he said. "I asked for extra dry. He gave me five to two proportions, unless I miss my guess."

"Oh, a connoisseur, eh?"

He shrugged. "You get to tell the proportions by the way the drink hits your tongue." Smiling, he waved to the bartender and said, "Mack, give the young lady an extra-dry martini, will you? The same kind you gave me."

Janey felt the warm glow of triumph, and it deepened as the man put a dollar bill down on the bar to pay for her drink. If she had gotten him to buy her a drink without even asking, all the rest would follow smoothly enough.

"Oh, no, you mustn't," Janey said as he paid for her drink.

"Don't worry about it, Miss, Miss—"

"Cartwright. Jane Cartwright."

"Jane. It's a nice name."

"Thank you," Janey said demurely.

They talked for a little while. His name was Ron Martin, he was an architect, he lived in Philadelphia, and he had come down to this resort city for a couple of weeks of fun and relaxation. He was, of course, unmarried. But that part was all right, she thought. If he came from Philadelphia, he would certainly prefer to pay up than to get involved in a scandal that might hit the local papers and ruin his architectural business.

She gave him the usual line—that she was a local girl, that her father was dead and her mother quite poor, that a Hollywood producer had once met her and promised her a screen test if she went to Hollywood, but she had never been able to afford the fare across the country.

Ron Martin ate it all up, nodding sympathetically at every

turn of the tale. Janey kept her eye on the clock, and as the time approached nine she began letting it be known less and less subtly that she was interested in going to bed with him.

Finally she said—she had had two martinis, he had had three, but every time he turned his head she had dumped a little of her drink into a nearby waterglass so she could remain sober and in control of the situation—"It's getting pretty crowded in here, isn't it, Ron? And I think I've had about enough to drink, at least for now. How about you and me clearing out of here?"

"Fine idea. Where to? A late movie? A stroll by the beach?"

She grinned conspiratorially at him. "How about upstairs?"

His room was on the sixteenth floor, with a big picture window overlooking the ocean. He had a double bed, though he was the only occupant of the room—so either he liked to have a lot of room when he slept, or else he had a lot of company in bed.

He drew the blinds, shutting off the view, and then pulled her to him for a passionate kiss. This was the best part of the whole routine, Janey thought.

She kept her eye on the clock by the side of the bed. At twenty minutes to ten she gasped and said, "I'd better get going! If I'm not home by ten-thirty my mother gets terribly worried, and her heart isn't so good—"

"Do you *have* to go?"

"Yes. I have to."

She dressed rapidly, now, three times as fast as she had dressed earlier in the day. There wasn't much time to waste. As she donned her clothes and tidied her hair, he said, "It was wonderful having you here—"

"I liked it too," she said, and she meant it.

"Will I see you again?"

"How long will you be in town?"

"Another week," he said.

"I'll meet you in the cocktail lounge at eight o'clock tomorrow night," Janey promised.

"I'll be looking forward to it."

"Me too," she said.

It was ten minutes to ten when she finished saying goodbye to him and left him in his room. Hurrying to the elevator, she rode downstairs and walked quickly up the block to the place where Charley had parked the car. He was waiting for her.

He looked unhappy, the way he always did when she came back from a session. He can't help feeling jealous, Janey thought. Even though he wasn't the first fellow she had made it with, he hated it when she cooped up with anyone else. Only the thought of the five hundred bucks made him swallow his jealousy.

"Well?" he said roughly.

"It worked fine," she said. "I picked up an architect from Philly. He was looking for companionship. I gave it to him."

"You took your goddam time about it," he grunted.

"I said I'd be back here by ten, and I am. So what are you moaning about? Come on, get this heap moving—we don't have that much time, you know."

"Okay. Okay."

He pushed the starter and got the car going.

Ten minutes later they were back at their own apartment. Janey rushed quickly through her transformation. Off came the low-neckline dress, off came the fancy-dan brassiere, off came the nylon stockings and the makeup and the sophisticated-looking hairdo.

Hastily she donned the outfit Charley laid out for her. A

cheap yellow sweater, tight against her body. An ordinary plaid skirt. Bobby-sox, loafers, a wide leather belt. She bunched her hair in a ponytail, put a different color lipstick on, and made a mental change of gears so she would be wearing a more innocent expression. The transformation was complete. In the space of ten minutes she had blotted years from her apparent age.

"How do I look?" she asked.

"Like a perfect bobbysoxer. All set?"

"Yeah. Just let me find the bubble-gum."

By ten-thirty they were on their way again, and by quarter to eleven they were standing outside of Ron Martin's room at the Boardwalk Plaza Hotel. She and Charley exchanged a glance. He looked nervous, the way he always did when they went to cash in.

"Go ahead—knock!" Janey urged him.

Charley nodded and rapped twice on the door.

"Who's there?" the architect's deep voice called out from within.

"Mr. Martin?"

"That's right. I'm coming."

The door opened. Charley pushed it open before Martin could do anything, and Janey followed him in. Martin was wearing only a silk dressing-gown. He looked puzzledly from Janey to Charley and back to Janey again.

"You ever see this girl before?" Charley demanded belligerently.

"Why, no! I mean—oh, *no!*"

"That's right," Charley said. "She was all dressed up before, but now she's in her everyday clothes. I made her change. A girl her age don't have any business dressing up the way she likes to."

"A girl her age?" Martin repeated, frowning. "Just—how old—is she?"

"She'll be seventeen next month," Charley snapped.

Martin looked bewildered. "This is some kind of joke you're pulling, huh? This is the kid sister of the girl who—who was here earlier."

"She's *my* kid sister," Charley said. "And she's the same girl you put your lousy paws all over. Show him the birthmark, Sis."

Janey had made a point of showing Martin the small birthmark on the inside of her left thigh. Now she hiked her dress up to her hips and sullenly demonstrated the mark again.

"See it?" Charley said. "It's the same girl. And not even seventeen. There's a law against that kind of stuff, Martin."

The architect chuckled. "But how is anyone supposed to know? I could have sworn she was in her twenties when she picked me up in the bar. And she picked me up, no two ways about that."

"It don't matter," Charley said stubbornly. "The law is supposed to protect young girls against themselves, too. It don't matter who picked who up. You went to bed with her, and that makes you guilty of statutory rape."

The architect stared expressionlessly at Charley. After a moment he said, "Statutory rape?"

"You heard me. They can put you away a long time for that. And it makes a noisy splash in the papers."

"Are you going to turn me in?"

Charley shrugged. "All depends on you."

"Meaning what?"

"Meaning that I don't want my kid sister's good name to get ruined by being smeared all over the front pages. So I'm willing to let you get off easy."

"How easy?"

"Give me five hundred bucks in cash and get yourself out of town by tomorrow, and I'll forget all about it. Otherwise I go to the cops and tell them that you're the bastard who seduced my sister."

Instead of answering, Martin began to laugh.

"What's so damn funny?" Charley asked.

"Nothing, really. Except that this is such a good dodge I wish I'd thought of it myself!"

Janey and Charley exchanged uneasy glances.

"Huh?" Charley said.

"I mean, this business of sending the girl into a hotel to pick up wealthy-looking strangers, and then dressing her up as a teenager to milk some dough. It's a lovely idea! And you damn near fooled me, too."

Charley took a step forward. "Listen, mac, I don't know what you're chattering about, but I want five hundred bucks for what you did to my sister, or—"

"Listen yourself, mac. It's a good story and you put it over well, and she sure looks the part. Only a little common sense tears the whole thing apart. If your kid sister's as young and as innocent as she looks, where'd she learn to be so good in bed? That 'teenager' knows some pretty grownup stunts, let me tell you. And she puts on a pretty sophisticated act in a bar, too. So I'm not swallowing your story. Go tell it to the cops."

Charley was absolutely silent. Janey looked at him in surprise. This was the first time anyone had called the bluff. They couldn't go to the cops, of course. Martin wasn't guilty of a thing except going to bed with her, and there was no law against that. If he flatly refused to pay, they couldn't do anything.

Charley said uncertainly, "I want that five hundred bucks, or—"

"Or you'll go to the cops. So go to the cops, if you want to. Try telling *them* she's seventeen, and prove it. You got a birth certificate or something?" Martin laughed. "Suppose you two get the hell out of here, now, before *I* call the cops and have you both run in for extortion. It's been very pleasant talking to you, and it was very nice to get an hour in bed with your sister or whoever she is. Now scram."

Janey saw the anger flare up in Charley. "Why, you lousy—"

He came rumbling forward. He was three or four inches taller than Martin, and maybe thirty pounds heavier. He brought one big fist up, but before he could do anything Martin's right hand slipped between Charley's fists and landed a solid blow in the middle. Charley grunted and stopped advancing. Martin came in to attack him.

Charley was cut to ribbons. He had all the weight, but Martin fought with practically professional skill. His fists weaved in and out, round about the confused Charley, landing damaging blows on face, chest, midsection.

Charley's lip was split and bloody, his eye puffed, his cheek bruised, within a moment. He hadn't landed as much as one blow himself. Janey stood frozen, unable to do a thing, as Martin mercilessly battered Charley to a pulp and finally grabbed him by the shoulder and shoved him, tottering dizzily, out into the hall.

Martin slammed the door. Janey said, "Let me out of here. You hurt him!"

"He asked for it."

"Let me out. Why are you keeping me here?"

Martin stepped forward and his hand dug into her shoulder. "You've got a pretty good racket there, kiddo. It's too bad Charley picked the wrong customer to deal with. How old are you, really?"

"None of your damn business."

"How old are you?"

"None of your damn business."

Martin's open hand sailed through the air and collided with Janey's cheek. The impact nearly tore her head off.

"For the third time," he said. "Don't make me knock all your teeth out. How old?"

"I'm—I'm almost twenty-three," she said, stammering with fright.

"That's about what I thought. Though you make a very convincing teenager, in this outfit. Okay. We leave for New York tomorrow morning."

"New York? We leave?"

He nodded smilingly. "I was just handing you a line, about Philadelphia and my being an architect. I'm from New York. Down here on vacation. I'm not an architect, either. I'm—in a number of businesses. And now I've got a new one."

"I don't understand you."

"You will, soon enough. You have any family here? Are you married to that goon I beat up?"

"I was just living with him," she said faintly. "I don't have any family."

"Okay, then. You're coming with me. I'll set you up in my place in New York and we'll run this statutory rape gimmick for all it's worth."

"No—no," she murmured. "Charley and I—we were supposed to get married—"

"He's a nothing."

"I don't want to go away with you."

The so-called architect's face was suddenly menacing. "You'll leave with me or I'll fix you so you aren't good for anything, after this. You hear?"

Thoughts pinwheeled wildly through her head. She was afraid of this strange man, afraid of his strength, his cruelty. But he offered the mystery and adventure of New York, of money. Why hang around with—he said it, a nothing—like Charley, when she could go to New York? She wavered, half afraid, half tempted.

Suddenly the door burst open. Charley stood there, a battered, bloody, disheveled figure. There was a knife in his hand. He had gone back to the car to get his knife, Janey thought.

"Okay, you bastard," Charley muttered in a low, hate-filled voice. "You're pretty handy with your fists, aintcha? And you got cute ideas about my girl? Well, after I've carved you a little maybe you'll have different ideas."

He came forward, kicking the door shut behind him. Martin, unarmed, retreated into a corner of the room. He had gone very pale. Charley was like a hulking gorilla, moving slowly toward him with the knife.

"Nobody gets to beat *me* up like that," Charley grunted. "I'm gonna cut your ears off first. Then—"

"Keep away from me, you ape!"

Janey watched, dry-throated. In another moment Charley would reach him, would cut him up, and then the two of them would be free to leave. Suddenly she remembered the way Martin had been in bed, and the slick, smooth way he had talked to her in the bar. That was lots better than spending the rest of her life with a clod like Charlie, she thought.

The decision took only a second. She grabbed up the ornamental vase that was sitting on top of the television set and smashed it down on Charley's skull.

He dropped like a felled oak. She looked down, seeing the blood welling out of his hair.

"Janey," he whimpered. "Janey—you hit me—"

His voice died away. He was out cold. Martin snatched the knife from his nerveless fingers and put it in his pocket.

"I didn't think you were going to do that," Martin said in a hoarse voice. "I thought for sure that ape was going to cut me up."

Janey smiled. There was a strange, bright, new look about her. She looked down at the unconscious Charley. *To hell with him*, she thought.

"We leave for New York tomorrow," she said.

DRUNKEN SAILOR

Originally published in the October, 1958 issue of
TRAPPED DETECTIVE STORY MAGAZINE

Marty Bowman felt slightly scared as he walked down Broadway in his sailor's uniform, heading for the big bar on the corner at 42nd Street. Tony Donelli had told him he was sure to pick up a girl for the night there, and Marty hoped so. But he was scared. He had joined the Navy to see the world, like the posters said, and this was the first time he was seeing New York.

The bright lights of Times Square dazzled his eyes. He had never seen anything like them before, certainly not back in his home state of Nebraska. He had been to Omaha a couple of times, but Omaha was pretty small potatoes compared with New York.

He reached the corner and stood outside the bar, looking in. It was a big place, long, dim inside. He could see people sitting at the bar—other sailors, too—and girls. Other people were sitting at tables in the back. Marty felt a lump in his throat. He was nineteen, a big raw gangling blond kid, and he had never had a woman in his life. Tony Donelli had been kidding him about it on the ship, all the past months while they had cruised the Atlantic making a tour of the American defense bases. Marty wished Tony Donelli had come along with him tonight, this first night of shore leave in New York.

But Tony had insisted that he go out on his own. "It's the only way to learn, kid. The fledglings have to be pushed out of the nest. But you'll make out okay. I got faith in you, kid."

It was encouraging to know that Tony had faith in him. Tony Donelli was about thirty, a tough, lean-faced man who was on his third or fourth reenlistment hitch. A real sailor. He had been all around the world for Uncle Sam's Navy, and he knew all the angles, every trick there was in the book.

In the last month or so he had taken Marty under his wing, so to speak. He had coached him in what to do when he got to New York. *Good old Tony*, Marty thought warmly. *He really helped me out.*

Yesterday, before the ship had docked, Tony had spent an hour giving Marty his final briefing. He had told him exactly what bar to go to for a pickup, had told him how to know which girls were looking to be picked up. Tony had advised him to carry a lot of money—girls like to be impressed that way—but also to be careful with it. Marty had cashed in a couple of checks and had borrowed a little dough too. He had better than two hundred bucks, all of it in small bills. It made a fine thick roll in his wallet. It was sure to impress any girl.

A couple of people went past him and into the bar. Marty moistened his lips, then licked them again. He couldn't stand out here stalling all night. Tony was sure to know if he was telling the truth or not, when he got back to the ship. He had to go inside, pick up a girl, take her to a room.

He sucked in a deep breath and decided the time had come. He pushed open the door and went in.

The place was noisy. Some kind of jazz band was pounding away on a raised stage in the back. Marty was bewildered and confused by the sudden rush of noise and smell that came to him at once, the noise of hundreds of people talking and the smell of liquor. But he got control of himself quickly. He remembered Tony's detailed instructions.

Go to the bar first. Have a drink first thing. Loosen up a little. Then look around.

Marty found an open stool at the bar and slid onto it. The

bartender was a thick-set bald-headed man who looked at him inquisitively without saying anything.

"B-beer," Marty said.

A moment later he found a glass sitting in front of him—half full, with a couple of inches of foam on top. He reached for it.

"Thirty-five cents, sailor." Marty peeled a bill off his roll and slid it across the bar top. Only as he handed it over did he realize it was a five and not a single, but by then it was too late. The barkeep glared at him and made change with obvious reluctance.

Marty sipped his beer. Thirty-five cents for a glass of beer seemed awfully expensive. But this was New York, he reminded himself. Everything cost too much.

He looked around, next. Now was the time to find himself a girl. He tried to remember the things Tony had told him.

Stay away from blondes. They're all pretty phony and some of them will play you for all you got and then not come across. Redheads you can't predict. Better look for a brunette.

And don't pick one too young, either. A lot of them can get you in trouble. Look for a girl about thirty or so. Old enough to really know the score. She'll give you a good time and help you along if you don't know what to do.

No flashy dressers, either. You want a simple type. She'll be sitting alone, maybe, or shooting the breeze with another girl. Don't cut in on a guy who's already hooked a girl. You may get your guts chopped up that way. Just look around and don't rush things. If you find a girl, talk to her without coming to the point. If she asks you to buy her a drink, you got it made.

Marty sat back on the bar stool, looking around, thinking about all the things Tony had said. And then he saw the girl.

She was sitting by herself at one of the tables, drinking a cup of coffee. She had light brown hair and she wore a brown coat that didn't look new. By the fleshiness of her throat she looked to be about thirty. Tony had showed him how you could tell a woman's age by looking at her throat.

This girl seemed to fill the bill as Tony had outlined it. Alone. Brunette. Not too young. Not well dressed. *This is it*, Marty thought. He stared at her a minute, and then she saw him and smiled at him. It was a direct invitation. Feeling calm and self-confident now, Marty pushed himself away from the bar and headed over to her table.

She looked at him. "Hello, sailor."

"Hello, there. Mind if I sit down—Miss?"

"Glad to have you. Always looking for company."

He sat down. His stomach was fluttery now and his heart was pounding.

She said, "I'll bet you came in with the fleet yesterday. You on shore leave?"

"That's right. Just back from a tour of the Atlantic bases."

"Must have been fascinating. What's your name, sailor?"

"Marty. Marty Bowman. I'm from Nebraska."

She smiled, showing tobacco-stained teeth. A little of her lipstick had gotten onto her front teeth, too. "I once knew someone from Nebraska. My name's Margie. Margie and Marty. That's cute."

She laughed and he laughed with her. Then she said, "Want to be nice to me, Marty?"

"Sure I would."

"How about buying me a little old drink, then? A girl can get awful thirsty sitting here by herself."

This is it, Marty thought. *Everything Tony told me worked out the way he said it would!*

"What do you want?"

"Make it a Scotch and soda," she said.

He cornered a passing waiter and ordered two Scotch and sodas. The drinks arrived almost immediately—this place operated efficiently—and the waiter wanted immediate payment. Two-fifty.

Marty wanted to say, "Two and a half for a lousy couple of shots of whiskey?" But he didn't say it. Instead he pulled out that bulging wallet and handed the waiter three singles and told him to keep the change. He watched Margie's eyes pop a little as she saw how thick the wallet was. She didn't have to know that all those bills were just ones and fives, he thought. Let her figure they're twenties or fifties.

He didn't mix the Scotch and the soda, but put down the shot of liquor first and then drank the chaser, the way Tony had told him to do. Tony said it was a waste of good whiskey to mix it up with soda or ginger ale, concoctions like that. He noticed that Margie mixed her drink up and stirred it around, but he didn't say anything.

He bought some more drinks a little while later, and again downed the shot straight. He forgot about the chaser. He was feeling very good. His hand had crept across the table and he was holding hers, and the music in the background had created a very pleasant mood. He made a mental note that he had to thank Tony specially when he got back to the ship. Everything was working out marvelously, just marvelously.

It was about quarter to eleven when Margie whispered to him, "Listen here, honey. There isn't any sense in you handing over a buck and a quarter a shot for the cheap whiskey they sell here. Suppose we get out of here now. We can pick up a bottle of something in a liquor store and bring it up to my place for a little party."

Marty grinned. This was what he had been waiting for all evening. Tony had said, *Just wait and she'll ask you to come up to her place!*

"That's sure okay with me, Margie!"

"Okay, then, lover-boy. Let's get out of here."

He left a tip on the table even though he had been tipping the waiter with each drink, and she took his hand and led him through the thick crowd at the bar and out into the street. It was a warm night and Times Square was crowded.

Marty felt very dizzy and very very good. He was sure that this girl was a sincere and honest girl who had had some bad breaks in life. She had told him a little of her story, and it was a sad one. She had married much too young and her husband had left her after a year or so. She had had a baby, but the baby had died and she had gone heavily into debt paying the hospital expenses. That had been five years ago, but she still hadn't recovered from debt, and she was forced to live in a cheap rooming house while she waited for the man of her life to come along. It was a pitiful story; Marty felt deep sympathy for her, and he was happy that an understanding woman like this was going to be the first one he had had.

They went around the corner and found a liquor store near Eighth Avenue. The store was big and brightly lit and was doing huge volumes of business despite the late hour.

Marty said, "What should I get?"

"Ask for a fifth of bourbon."

"We were drinking Scotch in there, weren't we?"

He remembered that it wasn't considered healthy to mix your drinks in one evening.

But Margie said, "Yeah, but I'm tired of it. Let's get some bourbon now."

So he bought a bottle of bourbon. It cost him six dollars, but he didn't mind. Charge it all off to entertainment, he thought.

Outside, Margie said, "Okay, now we go to my place. It's just a couple of blocks from here."

"I can't wait!"

"You better let me carry the bottle, though. You look kinda wobbly."

"I'm perfectly sober," Marty protested.

Her apartment was on 42nd Street past Ninth Avenue, in a very shabby neighborhood. Marty felt pity for her all over again when he saw her little two-room place, with the kitchenette and the cracked mirror and the dingy draperies. How could anyone go on living in a place like this, year after year?

She pulled out a little table and opened the bottle of liquor. Putting two glasses out in front of him, she said, "I'm going inside to change into something more comfortable. You get started on the bourbon while I'm there."

"I'd rather wait till—"

"No, have a drink." She poured it for him.

He grinned at her and downed the drink while she went into the other room and closed the door. Bourbon was sweeter than Scotch and burned a little on the way down. He began to feel very strange. But Tony had said, *Be a good sport and do a lot of drinking. You can hold it. I've seen your kind of physique before. You can take more liquor than you think you can.*

"Good ol' Tony," Marty said happily to himself, and poured out a second drink. He had downed that and was working on his third when Margie reappeared.

"Thought you'd never get through in there," he said.

He looked at her.

"How do you like?" she said.

She was wearing a filmy pink dressing-gown which revealed a lot of what was underneath. She wasn't wearing anything under the gown. Marty could see the hint of firm, full breasts, long creamy legs, a supple body. Maybe Margie was getting along in years, but she still had plenty of body left, he thought.

"I like," he said.

"Have another drink."

He poured one for her and another for him. His head was starting to swim. He reached out to grab her, but she ducked away.

"Naughty, naughty! Have another drink first."

The level in the bottle *was* diminishing rapidly. Marty realized vaguely that he was drinking about two and a half shots for every one of hers, but he didn't care. He was perfectly sober. Hadn't Tony told him he could hold his liquor? He had another drink. And another.

His head rocked deliriously. Margie seemed to be circling in orbit around him, like a lovely sputnik. She put some music on and pulled him up to dance with her, and he wobbled around the floor, full of liquor and dizzied by her nearness and warmth.

"Margie—Margie—" he mumbled.

After a while the bottle was empty and the radio was silent. He was holding her tight in his arms and his head felt ready to explode.

"Come on with me," she said.

She led him into the adjoining bedroom and dropped him down on the bed. He felt her unbuttoning his uniform and then felt her warmth against him. It was all very nice, though he hardly knew what was going on.

"Margie—"

Darkness welled up around him. He felt very tired, very drunk, very happy.

He wanted to sleep.

To sleep.

After a while, he slept.

*

He didn't know what happened next. He was out cold on the bed, so he didn't see the girl pick up his bell-bottoms and pull out his wallet. Didn't see her take the remnants of the thick bankroll from it.

Marty didn't hear the knock on the door either. He didn't see Margie go over to answer it, nor did he see the lean, thin man in sailor's uniform come in.

Margie said. "He's asleep. Like a little baby, out cold."

"Let me see him."

The lean man looked down on the sleeping figure. He chuckled. "Like a little baby," he said.

Together, they pulled Marty up and stuffed him back in his clothes, Marty mumbled a little in his sleep, but he was too liquored-up to realize what was going on. They propped him up and buttoned his buttons, and then the lean, thin man slung the boy's heavy form over his shoulder and carried him out into the hallway and down the stairs into the street.

The sun had not yet come up, but it wasn't much before dawn. Marty was deposited gently in an alleyway a block away and stretched out there. He would wake up in a few hours, or maybe the police would find him first and take him back to the ship. It wasn't unusual for a drunken sailor to be found in Manhattan.

The lean man returned to Margie's room.

"You put him outside?"

"Yeah." The lean man stared questioningly at the girl. "How much do I get?"

She picked up the thick roll of bills she had taken from Marty's wallet. Sadly she said, "It looked like a mint, but it was all small stuff. I figure we got a hundred eighty-two bucks out of the kid."

"Not bad for a night's work."

"Not bad at all."

She counted out a pile of bills and handed them over to the man.

"There. Half of a hundred eighty-two is ninety-one bucks, on the nose. Fifty-fifty."

The man pocketed the money. Then he said, "I don't have to get back for a while. How about you and me having a little fun now?"

"Sure," she said.

A couple of hours later the lean man left. As he stood at the door, Margie looked up at him and smiled. "Ninety-one bucks. Pretty good for a night's take."

"Have I ever failed you yet?"

"Not yet, Tony. You're swell. Next time your ship's in town, send me another sucker, yeah?"

"Sure, Marge. So long—and take it slow."

Tony Donelli turned away, patting the bills in his pocket. Ninety-one bucks. He felt good about things. He wondered if there'd be some other kid he could give good advice to, the next time they were about to dock in New York. He knew a good bar to go to for a pickup.

NAKED IN THE LAKE

Originally published in the February, 1958 issue of
TRAPPED DETECTIVE STORY MAGAZINE

So I was going to have to kill Peggy. It sounded strange, put as nakedly as that: *kill*. Murder was a crime that involved other people. Never yourself. Only now, as I fumbled out my key and let myself into Peggy's apartment, I knew there wasn't any other way out.

She was waiting for me, wearing a pink housecoat, her blonde hair up in curlers, her face pale, without lipstick. She looked nice and domestic. Just like my wife, only ten years younger. Twenty-three, instead of thirty-three. A good clean kid.

Her eyes went wide when she saw me standing there. "Mike!"

"Hello," I said, kissing her. "Well? What did the doctor say? Yes or no?"

Color came into her cheeks in a gentle rush. Her eyes dropped. "Yes," she said.

"Yes? You're—"

She nodded. "Yes. I'm going to have the baby, Mike."

I sank down on the cheap sofa and stared at my hands. "I don't understand. We were so careful—"

"The way you sound, Mike, you don't *want* the baby. Or me. Is that true?"

"You know it isn't, Peggy," I lied. "I love you. And I want the baby. But—"

"But what, Mike?"

"My wife's sure to make trouble. She always does. You don't know Helen the way I do, Peg."

A ripple of anxiety passed over her smooth face. "She'll give yon the divorce, won't she? I mean, she wouldn't want to hold out, Mike."

I shook my head. "Helen's a funny woman. Sure, she'll give me the divorce. But she'll stall and stall and wait around. Anything to foul me up. She'll wait till the baby's born. Then there'll be the mess of finding a place where you can stay until the wedding, of getting the papers fixed up so the kid's legitimate, of—" I stopped. "Well, it'll all work out, I hope."

"I hope so too, Mike."

I glanced up, eyeing her. Her figure was still slim, inviting, with no sign of the distortion that the next few months would work on it.

"What doctor did you go to?" I asked.

"The one in Brooklyn. Like you said. I told him my name was Mrs. McAllister, like you said." Shyly, she indicated the cheap five-and-ten wedding band on her finger and blushed again. "I didn't want him to think—well, you know what I mean, Mike."

"Yeah. And he said the test was positive?"

"I'm in my third month," she said. "Definitely. I'll have the baby some time next winter. February, most likely."

Like hell you will, I thought to myself. But outwardly I just smiled sweetly at her as if she were my wife and not just a spare-time hobby I'd picked up along the way.

She touched the cheesy wedding band. "I'll be getting a real one of these soon, won't I? Mike, I love you so much—you'll see about the divorce, won't you? I—I want to get married to you before it starts to show. You know how I'd feel if—"

"Sure," I said tenderly.

She was silent for a few minutes. Then, in the roundabout way she always uses to preface such things, she said, "I had a little trouble paying the doctor bill. I wonder if you could—

give me a little, just to tide me over, Mike. You'd be a doll. A living doll."

We'd been through this plenty of times before. I took out my wallet and slipped two twenties out of the billfold, crumpled them up, and stuck them in her palm. Somehow Peggy never seemed to have enough cash. In the year since I'd met her, I figured I'd given her a couple of thousand in cash, a drib and a drab at a time, aside from all the money I'd spent on her. Well, it hadn't mattered much to me. Helen had plenty of money when I married her, and she was due to come into plenty more next year. I could write Peggy off as an expensive hobby, period. As long as Helen didn't find out where the cash was going.

I stood up and put my hands on her shoulders, lightly.

"Got a little surprise for you, Peggy."

"Surprise?"

"To celebrate the good news. I've booked a cabin upstate for us. Two weeks all alone in the woods—no wives, no neighbors, no tiptoeing and secrecy. Just the two of us. I've got it all arranged. My wife thinks I'm going on a boating trip with a friend of mine—a *male* friend. While I'm away my attorney will let her know the score. Maybe the divorce won't take long. We can get married in a month or so, maybe. It'll be a sort of advance honeymoon, up there in the woods."

Her eyes were wide and clear. "Oh, Mike, that's *wonderful!*" she oozed.

Yeah. Wonderful. A cabin for two—but only one of us was coming back.

Well, I didn't want it to happen. I tried to get Peggy to take precautions. But I couldn't let her have any babies, and I damn well wasn't going to divorce Helen and marry her. Peg's ten years younger and twenty pounds lighter than Helen, but she's also a couple million dollars poorer. I really didn't have any choice in the matter. Not at all.

I held her in my arms. *Peggy Armour, age twenty-three. Three months pregnant, and due to die in the next two weeks.* It was a pity. But it couldn't be helped.

Maybe if Helen had been a little warmer, I'd never have been driven to find a Peggy, and the whole chain of events would never have gotten started. *If.* But Helen had good looks and a million bucks. It was asking too much to expect a loving heart besides.

I reached our eleven-room place on the Island just before dinner time. It used to be the old Jesperson mansion, and in its day it was one of the swellest places out here. It's still imposing, though some of the newer homes in our section are even fancier.

It had been Helen's home all her life, and she always made me feel like an outsider in it. Which I was. Her dad had been a rich steelman, and she had been born in plush and raised in it. Just why she married me I never figured out, except that she wanted some variety, perhaps. Certainly there was nothing aristocratic-sounding about me—just an ordinary guy, a commercial artist who had never made much money and never would. Helen had the money. She inherited close to a million from her father, and there was another million-plus in trust fund cash falling due on her thirty-fifth birthday, which was fourteen months from now.

When I came in, the maid told me Mr. Berril was in the pahlah with Moddom Foster, and so I took the left-hand staircase and headed upstairs to say hello. Stuart J. Berril was Helen's business manager and investment adviser, and he had known her a hell of a lot longer than I had; his father had held the same post for her old man, and he had simply inherited the account.

They were sitting at opposite sides of the sofa when I entered the parlor, with a pitcher of martinis on the coffee-table in front of them. Berril, as always, was immaculate—a clean-shaven pink-faced man of about forty, very very fastidious about such things as the fold of his handkerchief and the knot in his tie. After a long day in the city and a long railroad trip home, I knew I didn't stack up—I was covered with city grime and needed a shave.

"Hello, you-all," I said.

Helen detached herself from the sofa and glided across the carpet toward me. She was wearing her blue dress, the low-cut one, and it clung to her for dear life. She was a fine-looking woman, Helen, but there was something harsh and angular and unloving about her that I didn't find in Peggy Armour.

She kissed me, aloofly, simply grazing my lips.

"Hello, darling. How'd everything go?"

"Pretty well," I said, walking into the room and pouring a cocktail from the pitcher. "Hello, Stu. You and Helen figure out a new way to bankrupt the U.S. Treasury?"

"We've been discussing a new investment scheme, Mr. Foster," Berril said primly. I'd been married to his client for six years, now, but he still hadn't unbent far enough to call me Mike. "It may be a handsome little deal."

"Stu figures it'll bring in a 9% return," Helen said. "And it's a cumulative proposition with a steadily increasing increment. All we have to do is amortize the—"

"Okay," I said. "Spare me the details. Stu, you're a financial wizard. I bow six times to you every morning before breakfast."

A quick false smile flitted across Berril's face, and he rose. "Well, I really must be getting along, now. You must be almost ready for dinner, and I'll have to make my train, you know."

I knew. I also knew what Helen was going to say.

"Stu, why don't you stay for dinner, as long as it's so late? It's foolish to rush back now!"

Usually he accepted. But I guess this time he caught the black look I tossed his way, because he smiled again and said, "Really, I mustn't. Good night!" And then he was gone.

I gulped down the rest of my drink. "I wish you'd get rid of him before I get home," I said. "I don't like him and I never have."

"Stu's very helpful. He's earned thousands for our family, Mike."

"He hasn't earned thousands for me!" I snapped back. "How much of that money do *I* see? Damn little! I'm just Mr. Helen Jesperson, that's all."

"Mike—"

"*Mike*," I mimicked. "What are you going to say? How long is it going to be before *my* name at the bottom of a check means something?"

"You get all the money you need, Mike," Helen said, coldly, "I've never denied you anything. But the terms of my father's will specifically state that control of the estate is to remain in my hands. So dad had some quirks about money; so he opposed the marriage. What of it, Mike? Does it matter who signs the checks?"

"Yes. You could transfer the accounts just like *that*." I snapped my fingers.

"You know I couldn't. The will—"

"The will was filed five years ago. No one would be the wiser if we changed part of it now. What would they do, take the money away from us? There aren't any other claimants."

"Stu would never tolerate any such illegality, Mike. Please, dear, be satisfied with the arrangement as it stands. Don't start the argument again."

"Stu would never tolerate, eh? So we get rid of Stu! I'm tired of having him pussyfooting around the place looking at me as if I were a gardener who accidentally had wandered into the master's quarters. And we don't need a manager for the money. We have enough, don't we? Let it sit there and gather interest. Why keep re-investing it? Why be greedy?"

Helen glared at me bitterly. "We've been through this a million times. Stu's an old family friend; I couldn't think of discharging him. And I'd never be able to think of my father's memory again if I just let the estate lie fallow, after all his hard work to build it. Mike, let's not quarrel tonight; I'm too tired. You get all the money you can possibly need."

"All right," I said, very quietly. "I won't argue. I need five hundred dollars, though."

"Right this moment?"

"Not necessarily. Soon. Tonight."

"Of course," she said. "Will you bite my head off if I ask you what for?"

I smiled. "I don't mind telling you. I'm taking a little hunting trip with one of the boys from the place. I figure to be gone two weeks. The five hundred is pocket-money to cover expenses."

I expected some sort of explosion, but it didn't come. All she did was smile with surprising sweetness and say, "I suppose you rate a little vacation, dear. And it'll do us both good to be apart a while. We've been fighting so much lately, Mike."

"Glad you understand," I said stolidly.

"When will you be leaving?"

"Wednesday morning," I said. "Everything's all booked. I just have to confirm the reservations."

"I'll have the check ready for you tonight, dear," she said. "Will five hundred be enough?"

I hadn't expected so much cooperation, but perhaps Helen was mellowing a little. Anyway, she was true to her word—I got the five bills. Early Wednesday morning I left, getting a more than usually warm goodbye kiss. I began to feel good about things. It had been swell with Peggy for a while, but I was getting tired of her schoolgirl simplicity; Helen was more of a challenge, an iceberg that needed defrosting. I realized I'd taken the easy way out of our relationship by finding Peggy.

Well, I'd be rid of Peggy soon enough, and I could go back to Helen. She showed signs of defrosting. Maybe, I thought, if I could only try to understand her a little more, to remember that she was born to wealth and so thought differently from a guy who fought his way all the way up and was lucky enough to marry a millionaire's daughter. Hell, what did I care who signed the checks, as long as I got everything I wanted? The Peggy interlude was just an interlude. When I returned, I'd still have Helen.

Peggy met me at the station, carrying her little suitcase, and I kissed her hello. She was dolled up in her best clothes—the clothes I'd bought for her, with Helen's money. She was jumping with excitement and chattered about our "honeymoon" the whole train trip.

I had made reservations in the Adirondacks—one of those expensive deals where you can rent a little cabin in the woods, complete with a tiny lake, scenery, fishing tackle, and enough food to last you the time you were staying. It was Hermit's Delight. No automobiles. no people, not even a proprietor on hand. I had paid in full beforehand, for two weeks, so there was no checking-out problem.

The first two days at the cabin were swell. The warm July afternoons gave way to chilly Adirondack nights, and we huddled together in the little bed against the cabin wall, clasping each other for warmth. I was going to miss Peggy, I realized. Never in her wildest days was Helen ever like this.

We swam, and I fished while Peggy watched, and we hiked

through the woods. There was no sign of anyone around. The nearest town was eight miles away, and there was a good healthy timber-stand between them and us.

The days passed. Wednesday, Thursday, Friday. Just the two of us. Peggy was making it hard for me to do what I came here to do.

She'd sit there on the little beach in her skimpy bikini and smile up at me and say, "Mike, it's going to be like this always, isn't it?"

"Yeah," I'd say, but my voice would be harsh. I had to pity her. She had wandered into one of the spiderwebs human beings build around themselves, and for her the only way out was death.

Her body was still lean, her belly flat; I had trouble believing there was new life growing in her. But I knew I didn't dare wait until it became obvious; the doctor's report had to be accurate. If she'd been lying, if this was all some bluff designed to fake me into divorcing Helen and marrying her, then it was even better; I wouldn't even have to feel sorry for the girl then. But the days slipped by, and Peggy grew tanner and more lovely, and there was nothing to do but swim and make love and swim some more. At least, I thought, she'd have known a couple of weeks of happiness before she died. The short, happy life of Peggy Armour, I thought.

The ninth day went by, then the tenth. And I made up my mind I'd better get about my business.

I had it all planned. The old *American Tragedy* bit. The lake adjoining our cabin was long and narrow, maybe a couple of miles long and plenty deep; I'm a good swimmer but I hadn't been able to find bottom at the middle, so it was at least twenty-five or thirty feet deep and maybe a lot more. Maybe as much as a hundred. I didn't think they'd find her too fast, not up here in the woods.

So I suggested we go rowing.

"I'd love to!" she said. She was writing letters. Of course, she had no way of mailing them, but she was writing letters anyway, to various girlfriends of hers. Maybe she figured on mailing them when she got back. Maybe she was writing them just for the hell of it. In many ways she was just an overgrown high-school kid, anyway. She had none of Helen's cool, *too*-cool sophistication.

She packed away her stationery box and clambered to her feet, stretching. Her tanned body was easy on the eyes, and I thought, *This is the last time you'll walk around on dry land, Peggy.*

She was wearing a yellow-and-black two-part swimsuit. She came running down to the beach and got in the front of the rowboat; I shoved it off from shore, wading a couple of feet along with it, and jumped in. The oars dipped into the water and the boat glided away.

She leaned back, draping her arms over her head so the fingertips trailed in the water, and let her legs sprawl out so her toes touched mine. I smiled at her and tugged at the oars. No one was in sight. We hadn't seen another human being or even a sign of one since our arrival.

"It's sure secluded here," I said. We reached the middle of the lake and I stilled the oars, letting the boat drift. The water was like glass, dark green glass that became progressively more opaque. There was no wind, and the sky was cloudless. A lovely day for dying.

"You know what I'm going to do?" Peggy said. "I'm going to sunbathe. It's all right, isn't it? I mean, no one can see?"

"No one in miles," I said. "Maybe a bird or two overhead, but they don't count."

She unsnapped her halter and wriggled out of the pants and

crumpled the swimsuit into a little ball no bigger than a handkerchief, sticking it away under the seat. She stretched out, eyes closed, nude, lovely. Her body was a warm golden tan except for those places where it still was pale.

"The sun feels wonderful," she said. "This has really been swell, Mike."

I looked at her, studying the long firm brown thighs, the creamy swell of her full breasts, the softness of her, the gentle roundness of the belly that held a child—*my* child. For a moment I wavered; why not let her live, I wondered. Why not let the child be born, get the divorce, marry her, instead of destroying child and mother, killing the loveliness that lay bare before me.

No, I thought. It was impossible.

Peggy's beauty would not last forever; the years would coarsen her fine features, the proud breasts would sag, the body would grow flabby. She would want more children, and probably get them. We'd never have enough cash to pay two months' rent in advance.

I shook my head. I had had all I wanted from her already; the thing to do was to quit while I was ahead. Helen was waiting for me, Helen who was cold and icy but at least changeless, and who would keep me from ever wanting any material thing.

There were plenty of pretty girls like Peggy around, I thought. And very few Helens.

The decision was made. There was no choice.

Carefully I stood up in the boat and made my way forward until I stood over Peggy. She sensed by the boat's motion that I had come forward, and, eyes still closed, she smiled.

I knelt carefully over her and kissed her, feeling her warmness against me, holding her to me for the last time.

"We're going to be so happy, Mike," she murmured.

"Sure we are. Sure."

I ran my hands over her smooth body in one final caress and kissed her. She shivered a little and drew me close; I backed away.

I took a measured swing and cracked the side of my hand against her adam's apple. She gasped; her eyes opened and she tried to say something. I hit her again.

Then I lifted her, pressed her warmth to me for the last time of all, and let her slip over the side of the boat. She slid gently into the water, without struggling, I hope without knowing what was happening.

She seemed to float just near the surface for a long time, motionless, graceful even in death, a lovely full-breasted statue of a woman drifting in the water. Finally she began to sink. I watched her.

Her naked brown body looked curiously pale as it dropped deeper and deeper, and finally she was totally out of sight and gone.

So long, Peggy, I said to myself, and began to row back to the cabin...alone.

The rest of it wasn't as hard to do, but it took a great deal more care. I gathered up as much of her stuff as I could—the swimsuits, the lace-trimmed underwear, the bras and play shorts and the stationery box, and got it all together in the middle of the cabin. Everything she had brought with her. It made a little heap in the middle of the cabin, and I scoured every inch of the place to make sure I had it all.

Then I went through the stuff and burned everything with her name or any sort of identification on it. I gathered the ashes together, put them in a little jar, and set them aside. After that I packed the remaining things into her suitcase, making sure I'd pulled off her nametag, and added ten or fifteen pounds of rocks from the beach, just in case.

There it was: a suitcase, and a jar of ashes, and that was all that was left of Peggy. I got back into the rowboat and rowed a quarter of the way across the lake and dropped the suitcase over the side. It sank fast. Another fifteen oar-strokes further on I heaved the jar of ashes over, watched it vanish in the depths.

I paddled around the lake a while, peering overside like a fisherman trying to smell out some good bass. But I wasn't looking for bass. I was looking for the girl I had killed and thrown overboard in this lake, and I didn't see her—which was good.

Back to shore, then, and I felt good—numb, in a way, but good. I felt sorry for Peggy, but in the long run I figured she was better off this way. I could never have married her, anyway.

A couple of days later I went back to the city, feeling tanned and refreshed and clean. I wasn't expecting trouble. Peggy hadn't had any relatives, she said, and no one knew she was coming with me on this trip. The reservation at the cabin had been in my name alone. The return half of her round-trip ticket had been burned and now lay in a jar of ashes at the bottom of the lake. It was too bad I couldn't brag about it, but it certainly looked like I'd committed a perfect crime. Peggy Armour had just vanished, and no one would miss her, no one would ever find her body. Perfect.

That's what I thought. Until I got back to the city and found how wrong I was.

Helen gave me the big welcome-back treatment. I almost thought she was genuinely glad to see me. Naturally, Berril was in the house when I got out of the cab and came in—he had been going through some of her father's documents with her, he said—and he asked me if I'd enjoyed my vacation.

"Very much," I said.

"You look good," Berril said. "As if you got a weight off your back. You're looking very relaxed, Mr. Foster."

"Thanks," I said casually. I wondered if Berril was hiding something back of those innocent-sounding words. Well, I wasn't going to give him an inch of help. And I suppose I *did* look as if I had a weight off my back. A slim 110-pound weight that was at the bottom of an Adirondack lake, very naked and extremely dead.

Things went along well a day or so. Helen was nicer to me than usual, and the fellows at the office kidded me about my vacation. I felt good.

I hardly even missed Peggy. I knew I was going to miss those afternoons at her place after a while—but on the credit side of the ledger was the other stuff I had lost: the worrying about whether Helen would ever find out, the careful nervous inspections I had to give myself before entering our house, the sweat of transferring money to Peggy, the tension involved in waiting to find out whether or not she was pregnant.

That was one thing I couldn't figure, the pregnancy. I had always watched my step there, and yet it had happened anyway. Or at least Peggy had said it had. Maybe it had all been a bluff. In any event, it didn't make any difference now.

Perhaps you're wondering if I felt any guilt. Well, a little, I suppose. But at least the kid had been happy before she died. Up there in the woods she'd had more happiness than most of us ever get, including me. All I had done was spare her from forty more years of sweat and toil.

And then I got the phone call. It sure shook me up.

It came when I was at work, slaving over one of our most important accounts. I was bent low over the drafting board, planning my work three and four steps ahead, juggling seven or eight different compositional factors in my mind at the same time, when I heard someone come in to stand behind me.

"Excuse me, Mr. Foster. There's a phone call for you on Extension 103."

I glanced up with half an eye. It was Phil, the office boy. I said, "Is it my wife? Tell her I'm busy and can't come to the phone right now. Tell her I'll call her back in fifteen minutes."

"It isn't your wife, Mr. Foster. It's some man who wants to talk to you."

Berril, probably. He was the only man I knew who knew my office number. "Well, get his number, then," I snapped, irritated. "I'll be busy for the next quarter hour or so." I picked up my pencil again and turned back to my work.

"Got the number?" I asked when Phil returned.

"No, Mr. Foster. He wouldn't give it. Says he has to talk to you right now. He says it's urgent."

I scowled. Berril had a lot of nerve pulling a stunt like that, I thought. But I didn't have any alternative. I rose from my desk.

"Okay," I said. "I'll take the call. Thanks for the legwork, Phil."

I crossed the office, jabbed down the "103" button on my phone, and picked up the receiver.

"Hello."

"Mr. Foster? Mr. Mike Foster?"

I frowned. That wasn't Berril's voice.

"That's right," I said. "Who's this, please?"

"My name is Harrison. Duke Harrison." The voice was low and deep, confident, assured. I wondered who the hell he was and what he wanted with me.

It wasn't long before I found out. His next words were, "I'm a friend of Miss Armour's, Mr. Foster. Miss Peggy Armour. I believe you know her."

I nearly dropped the receiver. I could feel my face drain of blood. I looked at the phone wire as if it was about to turn into a viper. "Peggy—Armour?" I repeated slowly.

"That's right. You know her, don't you?"

I debated lying, then decided against it. "Slightly," I said. "Why?"

"I was just trying to find her, Mr. Foster. That's all. I was wondering if you knew where she might be. She seems to be out of town."

My stomach tried to crawl up through my windpipe and my mouth. I forced myself to say calmly, "I'm afraid I haven't seen Peggy—Miss Armour—for quite some time, now. I guess I can't help you, Mr. Harrison."

"You can call me Duke," came the slow, oily answer. "Tell you what, though: I'm really anxious to find her. What say I give you my address and phone number, and you get in touch with me if you hear from her again. Okay?"

"Okay," I said in a dry voice. I was beginning to smell shakedown here.

He gave me an address on the lower east side, and I scribbled it on a sheet of notepaper and jammed it in my pocket. "I'll let you know," I said.

"Thanks a lot, Mr. Foster. I'll be looking forward to hearing from you again. Soon."

The line went dead.

I dropped the receiver into its cradle and walked shakily back to my desk, having a little trouble getting there still standing up. Phil came over to me and said, "Everything all right, Mr. Foster?"

"Fine," I said. "Fine."

"You look kinda green," he said.

I chuckled hollowly. "That was my bookie. My horse didn't place. Don't ever gamble, kid; it's bad for the digestion."

"Gee," he said. "Sorry to hear that."

I didn't sleep so well that next couple of nights. I kept scanning the papers for the news that Peggy's body had been found, and every time the phone rang I jumped half a foot. I kept waiting for the maid to appear, with a faintly puzzled look on her face, and say, "Mister Foster, there's a Mister Harrison on the wire for you."

Harrison didn't call. I got jumpier and jumpier, though. I was starting to figure the possibilities, and I didn't like any of them.

Berril was around the house a lot, smiling smugly, using up our martini supply, eating dinner with us more often than not, working out new and better schemes for turning Helen's money into more money. He was a supercilious bastard if I ever knew one. Forty years old, a plumpish bachelor who got all his kicks in life from handling someone else's money. I was willing to bet he'd never been to bed with a woman in his life—or at least not in the last fifteen years.

Somehow having Berril around so much made me jumpier than ever. I made things rough on everybody, and Helen didn't like it. What was happening to that fresh start, I wondered?

It had seemed so simple: kill Peggy and all the clouds roll away. Just Helen and me, and no love-nest in Manhattan and no pretty little bosomy empty-headed bed-partner, and no worries about getting her pregnant. Simple. But it wasn't working out that way.

It was as if Peggy were still alive, only twice as bad, because now I had all the pressure and tension and none of the other things. I kept dreaming about that body floating to the top of the lake. I could see the big headlines in the paper:

NUDE BODY FOUND IN ADIRONDACK LAKE

And then the story, how the naked lovely had been murdered and dumped in the lake, and how medical examiners had found she was three months pregnant. And I could fill in all the rest of the steps. I had made my cabin reservation under another name, of course, and taken great care to throw red herrings along the path. But the police would start tracking down everyone who had rented that cabin during the summer and trying to link him with Peggy Armour. And there was some guy named Harrison who could tip them off to me, I thought.

I could see the next headline too:

HEIRESS' HUSBAND INDICTED FOR MURDER

But then I tried to figure it the other way—that even if they found the body, which wasn't likely, they'd have trouble identifying it after the lake got through with her. And even if they identified it, they'd still have a tough time linking *me* with the crime. Yes, I thought. It wasn't as bad as I was figuring. I'd squeeze through. I might live the rest of my life under the shadow of fear, turning away every time I saw a policeman coming up the street, but I'd get through.

I thought.

Until Harrison phoned again.

This time it was at home, and it happened to be the maid's night off. Helen and I were sitting in the parlor; she was reading some best-seller and sipping a drink, and I was staring at the daily newspaper without seeing too much of it. We hadn't been talking much to each other. Helen and I didn't talk too much, except when we were quarreling, which was only about half the time.

The phone rang. That was funny, we don't get too many calls, except from Berril, and he had left a couple of hours before. We both looked up.

"I'll get it," I said hastily, before Helen had even made up her mind about it. It was as if I *knew* who it was going to be.

I was right.

I snatched up the phone on the third ring and nearly shouted "Hello!" into it.

The calm, familiar voice said, "Mr. Foster, this is Duke Harrison. How have you been?"

"Harrison?" I bluffed. "I'm afraid I don't—"

"Yes, you do. A friend of Peggy Armour's, remember? I spoke to you just three or four days ago, at your office? Eh?"

"Oh—yes, I recall now," I said. I was praying desperately that Helen hadn't picked up the extension phone. If she were listening—I began to sweat. "I'm afraid I haven't come up with any information about Miss Armour since I spoke to you," I said. "And now if you'd excuse me—we have some guests here—"

"Just a second, Mr. Foster," he said evenly. "Don't hang up."

"I've told you I have no information. I hardly knew Peg—Miss Armour—at all." I picked up the phone and dragged the wire its full length, so I could peer out of the alcove into the parlor. Helen was still sitting there, reading unconcernedly. That was some small relief, anyway. "I haven't seen Miss Armour in months. I'd appreciate it if you'd look elsewhere for her, Mr. Harrison."

There was a moment's silence at the other end, and I wondered if he had hung up. But he said, after a long pause, "I think it's time I put matters squarely on the line to you, Foster."

I blinked. I knew what was coming. "What are you talking about?" I asked.

"I happen to know that you and Peggy took a cozy little trip upstate a couple of weeks ago. Also that you and she had been shacking up for quite some time. Also that she was expecting a baby. And also—that she didn't come back from the Adirondacks with you."

There weren't too many different things I could say in answer to that. I picked one.

"You're crazy," I said. "And if this is a blackmail stunt, I—"

He broke in smoothly with: "Point one, I'm *not* crazy and point two, this *is* a blackmail stunt. It so happens that I have a good chunk of documentary proof in my possession, including the late Miss Armour's diary. I knew Peggy pretty well. I also have some photos of yourself you gave her, and a few letters. It makes a nice neat little package."

"What do you want, Harrison?"

"Twenty thousand dollars, deliverable in one week or less. You have my address. I want it in small bills, because it's hard to cash $20,000 checks."

"And if I don't come across?"

"Then I mail the package to the police, with a little note telling them they'd better start draining a certain lake in Upper New York State. And just to make things nicer I'll send photostats of the whole works to your wife, so she can think twice about you before she hires a fancy lawyer to defend you. On the other hand, you can pay me and I'll guarantee to vanish without singing."

My hands were quivering. I said, "I don't have $20,000 lying around."

"Your wife does. Get it from her."

"I can't!"

"That's your problem, Foster. But let me tell you this: I sort of liked Peggy myself. I wouldn't mind seeing the twenty grand —but I'd be just as happy if it didn't come through, and I could turn in the rat who murdered her. Take your pick. So long, Foster."

I was holding a dead phone.

I stood there frozen a minute or so. I couldn't just walk back into the parlor and say to Helen, "Dear, I need twenty thousand dollars in a hurry, to pay off a guy who's blackmailing me. You see, there was this girl I was seeing on the side, and I—"

No. I couldn't do that.

Helen called in, "Mike, are you off the phone yet?"

"Yes," I said. My voice was so strained it sounded like somebody else's.

"That's good. Anything important?"

"Just some office stuff," I told her. "Some guy who can't make up his mind which end is up and has to ask advice. Nothing much."

"Bring in the ice cubes when you come back, will you, Mike?"

I brought in the ice cubes and put them down in front of her. I poured myself a stiff drink and tossed it down like cough medicine. The stuff was good, but didn't help to melt the cold hard knot of fear that was forming inside me.

Twenty thousand dollars. In a week.

And I had no way of knowing whether Harrison would keep his word after all. Suppose he took the money and then turned me in anyway?

The hell with that. I had to take my chances. And I had to get the money. Right now.

There was only one place I could get it.

I said, "Helen, put down the book a minute, won't you?"

She frowned and stuck a placemaker in. "Something on your mind, dear?"

"Yes. This business of the bank accounts being in your name."

"Mike, if you're going to start that *again*—!" She reached for her book.

"We've been married six years," I said. "Seems to me I ought to start wearing the pants around here. What happens if I need a lot of money suddenly—I have to come crawling to you, don't I? I'm sick of it! I feel like I'm being *kept*."

Color rose to her cheeks. "Mike!"

"Well, that's how it seems sometimes."

"I can't alter the will. You know you can have all the money you need, Mike."

I took a deep breath. "Can I?"

"Have I ever denied you, Mike?"

"All right," I said. I leaned forward in the big plush chair and knotted my hands together. "Helen, I want twenty thousand dollars by the end of the week."

"Twenty thou—Mike, whatever for?"

I smiled coldly. "Call it an investment. It's important to me. I need the money. Can I have it?"

I saw her frown suspiciously. This was the test, I thought. Now she'd have to put up or shut up.

"It's quite a lot of money, Mike. We don't have unlimited funds, dear."

"Twenty thousand bucks can't even be seen when you stack it up against a million. You'll never miss it. And I need it."

"What sort of investment is this, dear?"

Savagely I mimicked her: "*What sort of investment is this, dear?* You see? You see? You talk about letting me have all the money I need—but the one time I really need it, you forget all the things you said!"

"Mike, I never said you couldn't have the money. But so much, and so suddenly—why, I'd have to talk to Stu just to find out if we can spare so much at such short notice."

That was the topper. Speak to Stu! I rose angrily. "Okay, speak to Stu. But here's your chance to back up all those pretty words of yours with dollars, Helen. Here's your chance."

I turned on my heel and headed out of the parlor toward my bedroom.

There wasn't much sleep for me that night.

I got my answer the next day, from Helen.

She said, "I spoke to Stu about—your request. He says no."

"No?"

She nodded. "He told me we just don't have that much fluid cash on hand now. He's swinging some big deal that's tying up our liquid assets right now and he just doesn't see how he can pry loose a chunk of money that big."

It was a lie. A cold flat conscienceless lie. I knew enough about the Jesperson estate to know that $20,000 could be detached every day for a week, and twice on Sunday, and there'd still be some cash left over for tips. But I couldn't say that to Helen. I couldn't say, Did you really ask him, or are you just determined to put me in my place and keep me there?

And I couldn't say, Go ahead, play your games, but a week from now the police are going to dredge a girl's nude body out of the lake and burn me for it.

Instead I said, "I'll talk to Stu. Maybe I can swing it, if I oil him up."

"Don't, Mike. It's no use—"

"Let *me* try," I said, and phoned Berril's office.

He sounded cheerful enough, until I got around to the part where I asked for the money.

"Oh," he said, and I could hear the phony professional amiability drain out of his voice. "Hasn't Mrs. Foster spoken to you about that?"

So it was true, then. "Yes," I said. "But maybe she didn't make the matter sufficiently clear. It's quite an emergency. I was hoping—"

"I'm sorry, Mr. Foster. *We're* undergoing a bit of an emergency ourselves. Nothing too serious, of course—we stand to profit by it considerably—but money is going to be tight a little while. If your business venture could wait, say, three or four weeks—"

"No," I said, in a dead voice. "I guess it can't wait. Thanks, Berril. Do the same for you some day."

I hung up.

That was the way it stood. I had maybe a thousand dollars in my private savings account, no more than that; Helen had always been good for cash when I needed it, so I hadn't bothered to put much away. Only now Helen *wasn't* good for cash.

And I needed twenty grand in six days.

Five days. Four.

Harrison called with three days to go—this time, at the office again. The guy seemed to take a sadistic delight in shattering my nerves.

"Well, Foster? How much cash do you have raised so far?"

"Not a hell of a lot. Go crawl into your hole and leave me alone, Harrison."

"In three more days," he said smoothly. "The deadline's midnight Thursday. When my watch says 12:01, that bundle goes into the mail addressed to the police—and you can take it from there."

"I've got three days. Don't bother me till then."

❀

But the days passed, one, two, three. Time was streaming through my fingertips and I couldn't hold it back.

Twenty thousand bucks. Helen's *No* was final, and Berril backed her up. I thought of all sorts of impossible schemes— forging a check, borrowing the money from a bank, stealing it—but I scrapped them all. There wasn't one method among them that wouldn't eventually bring the law down on me, and I didn't want that.

Then the idea came, and I was surprised I hadn't thought of it long before. There was one way of solving the problem, simply, cleanly.

I would kill Harrison.

It was logical. If I got to him in time I'd be able to destroy all the evidence, and I'd be home free. If I got caught—well, they can only execute you once. Harrison's evidence already had me frying for Peggy's murder; I had nothing to lose and a lot to gain by taking him along with me.

Maybe. There were a million maybes.

On the deadline day I called home and told Helen I wouldn't be home for dinner.

"That's too bad," she said. "Stu came over, and he's going to be eating with us tonight."

"Well, the two of you have a grand time," I told her. "I'll be home late."

I had brought the hunting knife to work with me in my brief- case that morning—a gleaming deadly tooth, sharp and silent. Already I could see it plunging into the startled Harrison's throat.

He said he'd be waiting at his place the entire day of the deadline. Well, I'd have a little surprise for him, I thought.

The day dragged interminably, and I spent most of it shut- tling between the water-cooler and the men's room. At last five o'clock came. I packed up and left, ignoring someone's offer to ride to the station.

I went downstairs and had a hamburger. It was dry and tasteless, or maybe that was just the way my throat felt. I caught the BMT and took it downtown to the address Harrison had given me.

It was an old apartment building, way over on the lower east side, in a neighborhood that had been shabby fifty years ago and wasn't improved much today. I checked the number on the house against the note I had scribbled, making sure it was the right one. My heart kept trying to thump up into my mouth.

My mind wandered back and picked up the image of Peggy, alive and naked and desirable in the rowboat. I had killed her calmly, casually, without a moment's nervousness. I could see her body turning over and over, drifting slowly down to its grave.

But this was different. Funny; second time should have been a lot easier. But it wasn't.

There was no elevator. Harrison was in apartment 6-A, and I walked up the filthy stairs to the sixth floor, prowled around the dark, dank-smelling landing for a while, and found the right door. I looked around. No one in sight anywhere. I took the hunting knife from my briefcase, gripped it tightly, and knocked.

I waited for Harrison to open the door. I wondered if he was a short man or a tall one—I didn't know where to aim my thrust. But there was no answer.

"Harrison?" I knocked again. "It's me. Foster."

Still no answer.

"Hey, wake up! I've got something you want, Harrison!"

I pounded on the door again, but without getting any response. Maybe he went out for supper, I thought. I eyed the door. It was old and feeble looking. Suppose I broke it down, I thought. Suppose I got inside there and found the little package and destroyed it—or else just waited for Harrison to come back.

I put my shoulder to the door and heaved—once, twice. On the third heave the hinges groaned and gave way with a dry splitting sound, and I found myself inside.

There was no one there.

There hadn't been anyone there for a couple of days.

The place had been cleaned out. The dresser drawers hung open, the closet was empty, the bed unmade. A shockwave ran over me. What the hell—

There was a circular unpainted table in the middle of the room, with a piece of paper lying on it. Numbly I walked toward it.

It was a note. There was dust on it—two days' dust or more. I picked it up.

It was scrawled in pencil. I read it.

Monday night

Dear Punk:

After I spoke to you today I thought things over and I figure I'm not going to get any dough out of you. I also figure you're the kind of guy who might just as well kill a second time, as long as he's done it once.

So I'm clearing out, now. You won't be able to find me anywhere. I can get along without your twenty grand, even if you did dig it up, which I doubt. I'll be happy to know you'll fry for killing Peggy.

I left the packages in the Post Office—one for the cops, one for your wife. They'll get mailed. And you'll get what's coming to you, buster.

Here's one little thing for you to chew over on your way

to the chair: you weren't the first guy in Peggy's life. Neither was I. But that wasn't your kid she was carrying—it was mine. We did all right on the cash you gave her too. Then you had to louse things up. But you'll pay, boy. You'll pay.

I think I went crazy for a couple of minutes. I know I ripped the note up, and I may have busted some of the furniture. So all Peggy's fancy talk about wanting to marry me had been just a dodge, a way of squeezing more cash out of me. Helen's cash.

And the baby. Yeah, she was pregnant. But not by me. We took precautions.

For the first time I was glad I'd killed her.

But now I had to run, and run fast. The package would be getting to the police soon enough, I thought. I yanked out my wallet. Eight bucks. That wouldn't get me anywhere.

But there was five or six hundred in the wall safe at home— no fortune, but enough to get me out of New York, maybe out of the country on a banana boat or something. I didn't know. All I knew was I had to run, and fast.

I got out of there and took a cab to the railroad station; There I caught the 7:52 and sweated out the long ride home. It seemed to me the cops would get me any minute —that I'd feel an arm on my shoulder as I sat in the train.

But I didn't. I wondered when the evidence had been mailed, whether Helen knew, whether the police knew or not. I couldn't risk it. I had to run.

Funny: your whole world can explode around you in an hour, or a minute, or a second. That's what had happened to Peggy Armour aboard that rowboat, and now that was what was happening to me.

I took another cab from the station to the house and slipped in the back way. The lights were on, upstairs, but I didn't care to see anybody. I dashed into the downstairs dining room and yanked the big Monet off the wall.

The safe was back there. And I knew the combination. Helen had at least told me that.

It took three sweaty-fingered minutes to make the safe swing open, counting a couple of false starts. I finally had to stop, take a deep breath, and turn the knob in slow motion. I heard the tumblers click. The lock opened.

I reached in and pulled out a sheaf of bills. Five, six, seven hundred. Good, I thought. Torrents of sweat ran down my body. With seven hundred I could get away…anywhere. Anywhere.

I stuffed the money into my pocket. I didn't plan to take anything else—no clothes, no papers, nothing. I just wanted to get out with my skin intact.

I started to leave.

The lights went on.

I turned and saw Helen standing by the switch, looking icy and statuesque in her clinging gown, and Berril was right behind her.

"Mike? You didn't tell me you were coming home so early. I thought—"

"I changed my mind," I said. I saw them eyeing the picture propped against the wall, the open safe, but they weren't saying anything.

"We thought there was some prowler down here," Berril said. "This is the maid's night off, you know. We were quite startled."

"I'll bet you were."

I started to move toward them. They were blocking the doorway, I saw.

What the hell were they up to?

"Mike, you look awfully funny," Helen said. "Are you in some kind of trouble?"

"No—no trouble. But I have to get out of here. Let me get past, Helen."

I moved past her, but Berril was still in my way.

"Stu, get out of the way before I poke you."

"Mr. Foster, I—"

His face was pale and drawn. So was Helen's.

I heard a siren wail. A car pulled up. The doorbell rang.

Berril stood squarely in my path. I grabbed him by his padded shoulders and hurled him to one side; he bounced soggily off the wall and started after me as I raced down the hallway to the front door.

I opened it. There were three policemen there.

They stepped inside without giving me a chance to squeeze past, and I saw the dull blue glint of drawn guns. I heard Helen gasp behind me.

"This the Foster residence?" one of them asked. "And yes, we have an entry warrant."

"I'm Mrs. Foster," Helen said. "And that's my husband over there. Would you mind telling me—"

"Got a pickup order for Michael Foster," the cop said. "Suspicion of murder."

"You're mad!" I snarled, trying to wriggle loose. "Me—a murderer?"

"I don't know anything, friend. But you're accused of the murder of a Miss Peggy Armour. Pickup order just came through, and we have to bring you in. I'm sorry about this, Mrs. Foster. Just doin' a job."

The handcuffs appeared magically and slipped around my wrists. In panic I said, "Helen! Stu! Get a lawyer, fast! This is serious business!"

"I know, Mike," Helen said. "We got a little package in the afternoon mail. But we'll do our best to help you out. Won't we, Stu?"

"Of course," Berril said soapily.

"Come along, now," the cop ordered.

They started to half-drag me toward the door. The web was complete, now. Peggy and her Harrison, Helen and Berril—and me, scraped off on the ragged edge in between.

"I didn't do it!" I shouted, but it was the desperate automatic protest of a man who knows he's doomed. As I left the mansion for the last time, I squirmed round and caught one last glimpse of my wife and Berril.

They were watching my departure with keen interest. They were holding hands. And laughing.

ONE

It was cold out at Chicago International Airport. A chill, nasty wind was rolling in off the lake. I puffed on a butt and watched the big DC-8 come taxiing in. The three Chicago detectives grew tense.

"There she is," one of them murmured. "Flight 180, out of L.A. With Vic Lowney on board."

"Not for long," another chuckled.

I didn't say anything. It wasn't my place to make small talk. Leave that for the locals. I had a job to do, and the job began with my getting on that plane wearing Vic Lowney's name and Vic Lowney's identity. I only hoped the three locals didn't mess things up getting Lowney off the plane. One fumble, one bit of gunplay, and the whole job would be bollixed.

The DC-8 was slowing to a halt now. The ground crew went bustling out. They shoved the ramp up under the plane's door, and a moment later the passengers started getting off. A stewardess was reminding everybody, "Back in your seats in twenty minutes, please. This is only a brief stopover."

Two by two they came out. Los Angeles to Philly, via Chicago. I clicked off each face as it appeared. The twelfth man out of the plane was our man.

Lowney had a Los Angeles look about him. He was tall and broad and heavily tanned, and he stepped off the plane with a kind of a swagger. His thick black hair was shiny with pomade. He wore a bright yellow shirt, a string tie, pegged pants, suede shoes, and—though it was a gloomy afternoon in Chi—dark sunglasses.

If he could have seen me, lounging against the wall just inside the departure shed, he would have had a shock. The faces weren't the same, but everything else was. String tie, yellow shirt, sunglasses and all. I even had my cigarette drooping at the same angle. The tan had taken me four days under the U-V lamp.

I'm sort of a chameleon that way. It's what I get paid for. Right now I was busy convincing myself that *I* was Vic Lowney, number three man of the Southern Cal crime syndicate. Inside of five minutes, I was going to have to convince the rest of the world that I was Lowney, too. And my life depended on making it come off.

The three Chi detectives flashed their badges at the airline man and moved out onto the field just as Lowney came sauntering across. He had long legs, and he wanted to stretch them a little before resuming his flight to Philadelphia. The Chi boys might have been ad men right off Wacker Avenue, with their flannels and their attache cases. Lowney didn't suspect a thing right up until the moment they quietly surrounded him.

The whole thing took maybe fifteen seconds. They whispered to Lowney and one of them showed identification. I saw Lowney's face go icy. His lips moved in brief and probably impolite phrases. The Chi men murmured back, and one of them gently took hold of Lowney's elbow. He jerked free, and I thought there was going to be action, but the detective took the elbow again. They escorted him off the field, taking the next door down. I didn't budge. I stubbed out my cigarette and lit another.

Ten minutes went by, and then one of the detectives reappeared, smiling like a little boy with a report card full of A's. He wanted me to stick a gold star on his cheek, I guess. He said, "He's in custody."

"So?"

"Everything went smooth, no?"

"The plane's going to leave soon," I said. I'm not paid to hand out compliments to the locals. "You got anything for me?"

"Sure. Sure, right here."

He slipped me a little blue folder. Lowney's plane tickets and baggage checks. "When you get settled in Philly, go through his bags. Anything you don't need, turn over to the police. They'll ship it back here."

I scowled at him. I could figure out that much of the deal for myself. Slipping the folder into my pocket, I nodded quickly and slouched back against the wall. I didn't want to talk to him anymore.

From here on in, I was Vic Lowney.

I waited five minutes, and just before the other passengers started coming back on board I got in line with the people getting on in Chi, and passed through. I sauntered aboard the way Vic Lowney would. The stewardess gave me a pretty smile and welcomed me on board. I reminded her that I was a through passenger from L.A. That shook her up a little. The nose and the lips were all wrong, but the glasses hid the eyes, and the clothes were pretty much the same. I went to my seat. Lowney had reserved one in advance, and the stub was attached to his ticket.

The plane filled up fast. One by one, the engines started up. We moved out onto the runway.

Lowney had left an Angeleno newspaper on his seat. I picked it up and started reading about the Dodgers. A minute later, we were in the air.

I kept the paper open in front of me, but I wasn't really interested in the doings of Sherry and Snider and Gilliam. I was going over and over Vic Lowney's dossier in my mind, letting it seep into my brain until it became my own biography.

Your name is Victor Emanuel Lowney. Born 12 October 1927, Encino, California. Mother an Italian nightclub singer, Maria Buonsignore, died 1944 age 40. Father a movie bit player, Ernest Lowney, died 1932, drowning, age 30. You grew up in Pasadena, went to high school there, left in 1944 after three years. 1944-48, small-time crime. Car thefts, smuggling out of Tijuana, mostly girls. Met Charley Hammell October 1948. Originally hired as muscle, but quickly rose in the Hammell organization. For the last six years you've been his left-hand man. You have no police record, so he sends you all over the country as his personal representative. Like this trip to Philly.

You're a bachelor, and you've got a big house in Pacific Palisades. You hate filter-tip cigarettes, drink vodka martinis above anything else, and you've got a good eye for women. You eat steak for breakfast. You're hot-tempered but shrewd. You've made half a dozen kills, but nothing proven. You were rejected by the army in 1950 on account of heart palpitations, thanks to the special injection Charley Hammell's doctor gave you before your physical. In general, Vic Lowney, you're a cold-blooded louse.

I was used to being a louse. In my line of work you don't get to impersonate nice people.

You get word in Omaha or Fond du Lac or Jersey City that they need you, and next thing you know you're busy studying somebody and becoming him. Or maybe creating somebody out of whole cloth. It isn't pretty work, posing as a criminal. You swim through an ocean of filth before your job is done, and a lot of that filth gets swallowed.

But the job *has* to be done. *Somebody* has to do it.

I guess I'm the lucky one.

*

This time it was counterfeiting. For the past five or six months there had been a deluge of very classy queer stuff on the East Coast. Nothing but fives and tens, of course—it doesn't pay to make queer singles, while big bills attract too much attention. These fives and tens were pretty special. The engraving was downright flawless, and only the paper didn't quite measure up to Uncle Sam's own standard.

It was a close enough match, though, to fool anybody but an expert. Uncle Sam has a hard enough time keeping the budget balanced without competition from free enterprise. So the treasury men started tightening a net. It took three months to center the operation on Philadelphia. It took another two months to pick up the clue that Mr. Big of the queer-pushers was one Henry Klaus of Philadelphia, a man well known by the Philly authorities but thus far able to stay on the outside of a cell.

Picking up Klaus wouldn't help much. The way to smash the ring was to nab the engraver, who was obviously a man of great talent. Only Klaus kept him well hidden, evidently. Nobody had a lead.

At this point I got alerted to move into the case. The reasoning was that only an inside operator could get hold of that engraver. I was still trying to dream up a point of entry when we picked up word that Vic Lowney of L.A. was on his way East for a powwow with Klaus. The police had their own system of underworld intelligence—otherwise they'd never do better than parking tickets. They got the word. Lowney was being sent by Charley Hammell to line up a West Coast outlet for the queer stuff.

We got the wheels in motion. A West Coast man briefed me on Lowney. I roasted under a sunlamp to give myself an Angeleno tan. We plucked Lowney off his plane midway to Philly.

And here I was, twenty thousand feet in the air, wearing padded shoulders and a brand-new suntan and the identity of a louse.

It was getting close to five, Philadelphia time, when the plane started to dip low over the City of Brotherly Love. I fastened my seatbelt and waited for the landing.

It was October, and winter was closing in fast on Pennsylvania. The sky had a dull gray look, and the temperature was in the low fifties.

I strolled off the plane and into the terminal. This was the rough point, right at the beginning. The dossier said Lowney had never been to Philadelphia and knew none of Klaus' men personally. So far as we knew, no photo had been sent. The letter we intercepted mentioned only that Lowney could be recognized by the yellow shirt, string tie, and sunglasses. But if a photo *had* been sent—

I stood near the baggage counter and lit up. Two or three minutes went by. Then I saw two guys edging up. One was six-three high, and about the same wide. The other was small and ratty-looking. They both wore heavy slouchy-looking winter clothing. I ignored them.

The big one rumbled, "Uh—Lowney?"

I looked them over. "*Mister* Lowney," I said coldly.

"Yeah. We're from Klaus."

"*Mister* Lowney."

They looked at each other. I stared right through them. The ratty one said, "Klaus sent us, *Mister* Lowney. We've got a car waiting outside."

I made no comment on that. "Where's the john in this place?" I asked.

"There's one right around that bend," the big one said.

"Are you going to call me *Mister* Lowney or do I have to report that you boys are a bunch of crude yeggs?"

The big lad glowered at me. "The washroom is right back there, *Mister* Lowney."

"Thanks," I said. I pulled my baggage claim check loose and, handed it to the ratty one. "Here. I'm going to go comb my hair. Pick up my luggage. Two Samsonite cases."

"Yes, Mr. Lowney." I could see him gagging over every syllable.

I ducked into the washroom, gave my pompadour some fresh curlicues, and leaned against the wall and looked at my watch for five minutes. Then I walked slowly out. The reception committee was waiting by the baggage counter, and the little one had his foot up on one of my suitcases. When he saw me, he got his foot off. In a hurry.

"We got your bags, Mr. Lowney."

"Okay. You want a medal?"

"Follow us, Mr. Lowney."

I let them carry my suitcases. By now they had caught the idea that I wasn't going to get chummy with underlings. We marched out through the terminal to the parking lot, and up to an Imperial sedan half a block long. Why gang boys go for these big black limousines I'll never understand. They might just as well put up a neon sign that said *Gangster*.

The little man opened the back door and I got in. Pint-size tried to get in next to me, but I shooed him away with my foot.

"You sit in front, man."

The beady eyes were marbles of hate. "Now listen here, tough guy—"

"I said you sit in front. Want to debate it with me?"

His face unstiffened. He walked around to the front seat and got in next to the big one. I had taken the first round on points, by plenty.

"I'm staying at the Penn Plaza," I said.

"We're supposed to take you to Klaus."

"You take me to the Penn Plaza. You think I flew three thousand miles to run right into a business conference? Wise up, simps. I need some relaxing first."

"Klaus is gonna be awful mad—"

"I'll see him when I feel like seeing him."

The big boy turned around and said in a feathery voice, "Hey, *Mister* Lowney, you talk like you did us a big favor by coming here. You oughta realize that *we're* the guys who gonna do *you* the favor."

I gave him one cold look that wiped the smugness off his face.

"Can it, friend," I said quietly. "Are you going to take me to the Penn Plaza, or do I take a cab…?"

**Order BLOOD ON THE MINK today
from your favorite bookseller!**

Don't Let the Mystery End Here.
Try More Great Books From
HARD CASE CRIME!

Hard Case Crime brings you gripping, award-winning crime fiction
by best-selling authors and the hottest new writers in the field:

Five Decembers
by JAMES KESTREL
"MAGNIFICENT"—BOOKLIST, STARRED REVIEW

On the eve of World War II, a Honolulu detective finds himself
trapped overseas as the need to catch a killer turns into a struggle
to survive. *Publishers Weekly* says, "This tale of courage, hard-
ship, and devotion is unforgettable."

The Twenty-Year Death
by ARIEL S. WINTER
"EXTRAORDINARY"—NEW YORK TIMES

A masterful first novel written in the styles of three giants of the
mystery genre. Stephen King says it's "bold, innovative, and
thrilling...crackles with suspense and will keep you up late."

Charlesgate Confidential
by SCOTT VON DOVIAK
"TERRIFIC"—STEPHEN KING

An unsolved heist of priceless art from a Boston museum sends
deadly repercussions echoing from 1946 to the present day. The
Wall Street Journal calls this first novel "impressive, inventive,
and immensely enjoyable."

The Best of MWA Grand Master
DONALD E. WESTLAKE!

"A book by this guy is cause for happiness."
— STEPHEN KING

Forever and a Death

Based on Westlake's story for a James Bond movie that was never filmed! Millions will die to satisfy one man's hunger for gold—and revenge...

Double Feature

The movie critic and the movie star—how far would they go to keep their secrets buried?

Memory

With his memory damaged after a brutal assault and the police hounding him, actor Paul Cole fights to rebuild his shattered life.

Brothers Keepers

"Thou Shalt Not Steal" is only the first commandment to be broken when the Crispinite monks of New York City try to save their monastery from the wrecking ball.

Help I Am Being Held Prisoner

A gang of convicts plots to use a secret tunnel not to escape from prison but to rob two banks while they have the perfect alibi: they couldn't have done it since they're already behind bars...